Damn, what was going on here? Ray's brain demanded silently.

This was Holly, right?

He wasn't sure anymore but even so, he was fairly certain that it really couldn't be. This woman didn't dress like Holly, didn't act like Holly, and most of all, she didn't *taste* the way he'd always assumed that Holly would taste if he ever thought to fleetingly sample her lips.

The Holly Johnson he knew would have smelled of soap and tasted like some kind of minty toothpaste. Holly was practical. Holly was grounded. By no stretch of the imagination was she some femme fatale who got his pulse running like the lead car in the Indianapolis 500 and his imagination all fired up—like this woman did.

Dear Reader,

We've come to the last of the Rodriguez brothers. With all five of his siblings either married or, in Mike's case, about to be married, Ray Rodriguez considers himself to be the last man standing—and this enthusiastic playboy with a golden tongue fully intends to remain that way. He's having, he tells his best friend, too much fun to ever consider getting married. And that's unfortunate for his best friend, because his best friend is Holly Johnson, who has been in love with Ray since the first grade. As his best friend, she knows him better than anyone, is privy to all his secrets and, sadly for her, gets to listen to Ray talk about each of his many girlfriends.

When a series of events—not the least of which is having his sister Alma give birth in the diner's restroom, with Holly in attendance—cause him to look at Holly in a different light, he begins to wonder what took him so long to realize how terrific, not to mention beautiful, she really is. Now how to convince Holly that he's really serious and not just pulling her leg?

Got your attention? Good. Start reading.

As ever, thank you for that—and from the bottom of my heart, I wish you someone to love who loves you back.

All the best,

Marie Ferrarella

THE COWBOY'S CHRISTMAS SURPRISE

—

Marie Ferrarella

HARLEQUIN® AMERICAN ROMANCE®

Recycling programs
for this product may
not exist in your area.

ISBN-13: 978-0-373-75482-3

THE COWBOY'S CHRISTMAS SURPRISE

Copyright © 2013 by Marie Rydzynski-Ferrarella

Printed in U.S.A.

ABOUT THE AUTHOR

Marie Ferrarella, a *USA TODAY* bestselling and RITA® Award-winning author, has written more than two hundred books for Harlequin, some under the name Marie Nicole. Her romances are beloved by fans worldwide. Visit her website, www.marieferrarella.com.

Books by Marie Ferrarella

*Cavanaugh Justice
**The Doctors Pulaski
<>Kate's Boys
††The Fortunes of Texas: Return to Red Rock
()The Baby Chase
†Matchmaking Mamas
=The Fortunes of Texas: Lost…and Found
‡‡Forever, Texas
^Montana Mavericks: The Texans Are Coming!
#The Fortunes of Texas: Whirlwind Romance
-Montana Mavericks: Back in the Saddle
***The Fortunes of Texas: Southern Invasion
‡The Coltons of Wyoming

To
Charlie,
Who can still make
My heart
Skip a beat
Just by looking at me.

Prologue

The bouquet of flowers she'd given her mother for her birthday had done more than serve its purpose. The arrangement of yellow mums, pink carnations and white daisies had remained fresh looking and had lasted more than the customary few days, managing to dazzle for a little more than a week and a half.

However, now, as to be expected, the flowers were finally dying, no longer brightening the family room where her mother usually spent a good deal of her day. Their present drooping, dried-up state accomplished just the opposite, so it was now time to retire the cluster of shriveling flowers to the trash can on the side of the house.

But as she began to throw the wilted bouquet away, one white daisy caught Holly's eye. Unlike the others, it had retained some of its former vibrancy.

On an impulse, she plucked the daisy out of the cluster, pulling the stem all the way out and freeing it from its desiccated brethren. After dumping the rest of the bouquet into the garbage, she closed the lid of the trash can, then stared at the single daisy in her hand.

Holly shut her eyes, made a wish—the same one

she'd made over and over again for more than a decade and a half—and opened them again.

Then, very slowly, she tugged on one petal at a time, denuding the daisy gradually and allowing each plucked petal to glide away on the light late-fall breeze that had begun to stir.

"He loves me," Holly Johnson whispered, a wistful, hopeful smile curving her lips as she watched the first white petal float away. "He loves me not."

Just to say those words made her chest ache. She knew she was being silly, but it hurt nonetheless. Because in all the world, there was nothing she wanted more than to have the first sentence be true.

The petal floated away like its predecessor.

"He loves me," she recited again, pulling a third petal from the daisy.

Her smile faded with the fourth petal, then bloomed again with the fifth. With two petals left, the game ended on a positive note.

She looked at the last petal a long moment before she plucked it. "He loves me."

This petal, unlike the others, had no breeze to ride, no puff of air to take it away. So instead, when she released it, it floated down right at her feet.

Unable to live?

Or unable to leave?

She sighed and shook her head. What did flowers know anyway? It was just a silly game.

The next moment, she heard her mother calling her name. "Coming!" she responded, raising her voice.

Then, pausing just for a second, she quickly bent down to pick up the petal, curling her fingers around it. She pressed her hand close to her heart.

Turning on her heel, she hurried back into the house, a small, soft smile curving the corners of her mouth. The corners of her soul.

The last sing-song refrain she'd uttered echoed in her head.

He loves me.

Chapter One

"Hi, Doll, how's it going?"

Holly Johnson's heart instantly skipped a beat and then quickened, the way it always did when she heard his voice or first saw him coming her way.

It had been like that since the very first time she had set eyes on the tall, broad-shouldered and raven-haired Ramon Rodriguez, with his soul-melting brown eyes, all the way back in the first grade.

The beginning of the second day of the first week of first grade, to be exact. That was the day she'd started first grade. Looking to change his luck, her father had moved his family—her mother, older brother Will and her—from a dirt farm in Oklahoma to Forever, Texas.

Back then she'd been a skinny little tomboy and the only reason Ray had noticed her at all was because she was not only determined to play all the games that boys played, she was actually good at them. She could outrun the fastest boy in class, climb trees faster than he could and wasn't afraid of bugs or snakes, no matter which one was dangled in front of her face.

And she didn't care about getting dirty.

All those talents and qualities had been previously

acquired in Holly's quest to gain her older brother's favor. She never quite succeeded, because during their childhood Will had never thought of her as anything other than a pest he was glad to ditch. During those years, Will was only interested in girls, and he'd thought of her as just holding him back from his chosen goal.

Ray and Will, although several years apart in age, shared the same interest; but while Will had thought of her as a pest, Ray came to think of her as a pal, a confidante. In short, he saw her as—and treated her like—another guy.

Holly was so crazy about him she took what she could get. So over the years she got close to Ray as only a friend could, and while she would rather have had him think of her as a girlfriend, she consoled herself with the fact that in Ray's life girlfriends came and went very quickly, but she remained the one constant in his life outside of his family.

It was a consolation prize she could put up with until Ray finally came to his senses and realized just what had been waiting for him all along.

It was a decision Holly had come to at the ripe old age of eleven.

That was thirteen years ago.

She was still waiting.

There were times, Holly had to admit, when she felt as if Ray didn't see her at all, that to him she was just part of the scenery, part of the background of what made up the town. These days, because money was short and she had to provide not just for herself but for her mother and for Molly, the four-year-old Will had left in her care when he abruptly took off for places West, she worked as a waitress at Miss Joan's diner.

The highlight of her day was seeing Ray.

He stopped by the diner whenever he came to town—which was frequently, because he was in charge of picking up supplies for Rancho Grande, the ranch that he, his father, his brothers and his sister all owned equally. And every time Ray walked into the diner, she'd see him before he ever said a word.

It was tantamount to an inner radar that she'd developed. It always went off and alerted her whenever Ray was anywhere within the immediate vicinity. She'd always turn to look his way, and her heart would inevitably do its little dance before he called out his customary greeting to her.

Ray had taken to calling her Doll, because it rhymed with her name and she was a foot shorter than he was. She loved it, though she was careful not to show it.

"I'll take the usual, Doll."

The "usual" was comprised of coffee, heavily laced with creamer, and a jelly donut—raspberry. In the rare instance that the latter was unavailable, Ray was willing to settle for an apple-filled donut, but raspberry was his favorite, and ever since Miss Joan had placed her in charge of doing the inventory and placing the weekly orders, she made sure that there were always plenty of raspberry-jelly donuts on hand. It wouldn't do to run out.

She would have made them herself if she'd had to, but, luckily, the supplier she used for their weekly orders never seemed to run out.

Technically, Holly thought as she concentrated on

regulating her breathing and appearing calm, Ray wasn't actually coming her way. He was coming to sit down at the counter, get his morning coffee and donut and shoot the breeze for a few minutes. With any pretty face that might have shown up at the counter that morning.

Or, if he was particularly excited about something, or had something exceptional to share, then he'd deliberately seek out her company the way he always did if he needed advice, sympathy or a sounding board. Over the years, she had become his go-to person whenever something of a more serious nature came up.

This morning, Ray had some news to share with her. Big news, from his point of view.

"You'll never guess what," he said to her as she filled his coffee cup and placed the sweetened creamer next to it. Unlike his brothers whenever they stopped by, Ray hated black coffee. For him to be able to drink it, his coffee had to be a pale shade of chocolate.

Holly raised her eyes to meet his soft brown ones as she set down the half-filled coffeepot, waiting for him to continue talking.

He, apparently, was waiting for something, too. "You're not guessing," he prompted.

"You really want me to guess?" she asked, surprised. But she could see that he was serious. "Okay. But to do a decent job at guessing, I'm going to need a hint." With Ray, there was never any telling what he thought was share worthy at any particular given time.

He nodded, obviously enjoying stretching this out.

"Okay, if you want a hint, how's this?" he said just before he declared, *"The Last of the Mohicans."*

Holly stared at the face that popped up in her dreams at least three nights a week, usually more. What he'd just said didn't make any sense to her, but she took a stab at it. It really didn't matter all that much to her *what* Ray said to her as long as he went on talking. She loved the sound of his voice, loved everything about him, even his devil-may-care attitude, despite the fact that it was responsible for his going from female to female.

"You're reading James Fenimore Cooper?" she asked uncertainly. Why did he think the book title would mean anything to her?

"No, me," he told her, hitting his chest with his fisted right hand. When she continued to stare at him, a puzzled expression on her face, he elaborated a little further for her. "*I'm* the last of the Mohicans."

Holly knew that he had a little bit of Native American blood in him on his father's side, but he'd told her that he had traced it back to an Apache tribe, not some fictional tribe the long-dead author had written about.

"It's too early for brainteasers, boy."

Holly glanced up to see that Miss Joan had joined them, having made her way to this side of the counter. The red-haired older woman who owned and ran the diner narrowed her hazel eyes as she fixed the youngest of the Rodriguez clan with a reproving look.

"Why don't you just come out and tell Holly what you're trying to say while she's still young enough to be able to hear you?" Miss Joan suggested.

But Ray apparently enjoyed being enigmatic and he gave hinting one final try. *"Last Man Standing."*

"Ray," Miss Joan said in a warning tone, "you're going to be the last man sitting on his butt outside my diner if you don't stop playing games and just say what you're trying to say."

Ray sighed, shaking his head. He'd thought that Holly, whom he'd always regarded as being sharp, would have already figured out what he was trying to tell her.

"All right, all right," he said, surrendering. "You know, you take all the fun out of things, Miss Joan." He couldn't resist complaining.

In response, Miss Joan gave him a wicked little smile. "That's not what my Harry says," she informed him, referring to the husband she'd acquired not long ago after years of being Forever's so-called carefree bachelorette.

Meanwhile, Holly stood waiting to find out what it was that had her best friend so mysteriously excited.

"All right, *why* are you the last man standing?" she asked, prodding him along.

"Because everyone else in my family is dropping like flies," he told her vaguely, playing it out as long as he could. "Except for my dad," he threw in. "But he doesn't really count." Eyes all but sparkling, he looked from Miss Joan to Holly, then said, "We just had another casualty last night."

"Don't see why a casualty would have you grinning from ear to ear like that," Miss Joan observed, then ordered, "C'mon, spit it out, boy. What the devil are you talking about?"

The twinkle in the woman's hazel eyes, Holly noted, seemed to be at odds with the question she'd just asked and the way she'd asked it. Everyone understood that Miss Joan knew it all: was privy to every secret, knew what people were doing even before they did it at times and in general was viewed as a source of information for everything that was taking place in Forever.

"Don't tell me you don't know," Ray suddenly said, looking at the older woman. He was savoring every second of this—especially if it turned out that he knew something before Miss Joan actually did.

"I'm not saying one way or the other, I'm just saying that since you're so all fired up about spilling these particular beans, you should spill them already—before someone decides to string you up."

It wasn't a suggestion, it was a direct order, and if she actually *did* somehow know what he was about to tell Holly, he appreciated Miss Joan allowing him to be the one to make the announcement. After all, it did concern his family.

Forever was a town where very little happened. They had the customary sheriff and he had appointed three deputies—including his sister, Alma—but they spent most of their time taking care of mundane things like getting cats out of trees and occasionally locking up one of several men in Forever who had trouble holding their liquor. Occasionally the men in question had imbibed too much in their singular attempts to drown out the sound of displeased wives.

Moreover, it was a town where everyone knew everyone else's business, so to be the first one to know something or the first one to make an announcement regarding that news was a big deal.

"Well?" Holly coaxed, waiting. "Are you going to tell me or am I going to have to shake it out of you?" It was a threat that dated back to their childhood when they were rather equally matched on the playing field because they were both incredibly skinny.

He grinned at her. "You and what army?" he teased. When she pretended to take a step forward, he held up his hands as if to stop her. Having played out the moment, he was finally ready to tell her what he'd come to say.

"You know the woman who came to our ranch to work on that box of diaries and journals my dad found in our attic?"

Holly nodded. She'd caught a glimpse or three of Samantha Monroe, the person Ray was referring to, when she'd stopped by the diner. The woman had the kind of face that looked beautiful without makeup and Holly truly envied her that. She wore very little makeup herself, but felt that if she went without any at all, she had no visible features.

"Yes," she answered Ray patiently. "I remember. What about her?"

Ray grinned broadly. "Well, guess which brother just popped the question?" Ray's soft brown eyes all but danced as he waited for her to make the logical assumption.

For one horrifying split second, Holly's heart sank to the bottom of her toes as she thought Ray was referring to himself. She'd seen the way he'd initially looked at this Samantha person, and even someone paying marginal attention would have seen that he'd been clearly smitten with the attractive redhead.

And while she knew that Ray's attraction to a woman had the sticking power of adhesive tape that had been left out in the sun for a week, there was always the silent threat hanging over her head—and her heart—that someday, some woman would come along who would knock his socks off, get her hooks into him and Ray would wind up following this woman to the ends of the earth, hopelessly in love and forever at her beck and call.

But then she realized that the smile curving his sensual mouth was more of a smirk than an actual smile. She wasn't exactly a leading authority on the behavior of men, but she was fairly certain that a man didn't smirk when he was talking about finding the love of his life and preparing to marry her.

So he wasn't referring to himself.

That left only—

"Mike?" she asked, stunned as she stared at Ray. "Seriously?"

Miguel Rodriguez Jr., known to everyone but his father as Mike, was the eldest of the brothers. Unlike Ray, Mike smiled approximately as often as a blue moon appeared. If Ray dated way too much, Mike hardly dated at all. From everything she'd seen, the eldest of the Rodriguez siblings had devoted himself to working the ranch and being not just his father's right hand, but his left one, as well.

She'd just assumed that the man would never marry. He was already married to the ranch.

"Mike asked this woman to marry him?" she asked incredulously.

She'd known all the brothers for as long as she'd known Ray, but for the most part, she knew them *through* Ray's eyes and Ray's interpretation of their actions. According to Ray, while Mike wasn't a woman hater, he wasn't exactly a lover of women, either. And he had no time to cultivate a relationship.

Yet, as she recalled, whenever she did see this Samantha they were talking about, she'd been in Mike's company.

Well, what do you know. Miracles do happen.

Ray's news gave her hope.

"Yeah." Ray laughed at the surprised look on Holly's face. "Knocked my boots off, too," he admitted. "So right after Christmas—they want to get married Christmas Eve," he added, realizing he had left that part out, "I'll be the only single Rodriguez male walking around." There was laughter in his eyes as he relished the image that projected.

"Maybe that's because the girls in Forever have the good sense to know that as a husband, you'd wind up being a lot more work for them than most men," Miss Joan quipped.

"No, it's because I've got the good sense never to get married," Ray told Miss Joan, contradicting the diner owner. He leaned his head on his upturned palm as he glanced toward one of the tables where four female customers around his age were seated, eating their breakfasts in between snippets of the conversation they were engaged in. He sighed in deep appreciation as he looked at the women. "There're just too many beautiful flowers out there for me to pick to be confined to just a garden on my own property."

"So now you're a gardener?" Miss Joan asked, rolling her eyes. "Lord help us all."

She glanced over toward Holly for a moment, her look speaking volumes. But she said nothing further out loud before leaving to wait on the sheriff, who had just walked in.

"Morning, Sheriff," Miss Joan said, greeting him as she automatically applied a towel to the counter and wiped down an already clean area. "Have you heard the news?" She didn't bother waiting for him to respond or even make a guess. "The last of the eligible Rodriguez boys is getting hitched."

Sheriff Rick Santiago's expressive eyebrows drew together in a look of confusion. Alma, in between stifled groans as she lowered her very pregnant body onto her chair, had told him the news about her brother this morning. But this little detail that Miss Joan had just sprung on him hadn't been mentioned.

"The last?" Rick echoed. "I thought Ray was still unattached."

Miss Joan smiled complacently. "I said *eligible*, Sheriff," the woman pointed out. "That implies a good catch. Ray there—" she nodded in Ray's direction "—is the kind you catch and then release after you realize that there's no way he's going to be a good fit for that kind of a position."

Ray turned around on his stool to face the older woman. He looked more amused than annoyed as he asked, "Are you saying I'm not the marrying kind? Or the kind no one wants to marry?"

Miss Joan looked at him for a long moment, her expression completely unreadable, before she finally said, "Well, boy, I guess you're the only one who really knows the answer to that one, aren't you?"

Taking out a number of singles, Ray left them on the counter as he slid off his stool. The wrapped-up, partially consumed jelly donut was in his hand.

"Good thing I love you, Miss Joan," he said to the woman as he walked passed her. "Because you sure have a way of knocking down a man's ego."

Miss Joan shook her head, a knowing smile on her lips. "You're not a man yet, Ray. Come back and talk to me when you are," she concluded with a smart, sassy nod of her head.

"And you," she said in a low, throaty whisper as she walked by Holly. "Stop looking at him as if he was the cutest little kitten in the whole world and you were going to just die if you couldn't hold him in your arms and call him your own. You want him, missy? Go out and get him!" Miss Joan ordered the girl who'd been in her employ for the past five years.

Holly's eyes darted around to see if anyone within the immediate area had overheard Miss Joan's succinct, albeit embarrassing romance advice.

To her undying relief, apparently no one had. And the person who actually counted in all this was on his way to the front door—to run whatever errands he had for his father and to shoot the breeze with every pretty girl and woman who crossed his path.

Holly had no idea she was sighing until Miss Joan looked at her from across the diner. While she didn't think she was possibly loud enough to be heard the length of the diner, she did know that Miss Joan had the ability to intuit things and read between the lines, no matter how tightly drawn those lines might be.

She also knew that she owed a huge debt of gratitude to the woman. Miss Joan had offered her a job out of the blue just when she'd needed it the most and would have given her a roof over her head if she'd needed that, as well.

It was Miss Joan who had taken an interest in her and encouraged her to take some courses online, following up on her dream to become a nurse, specifically, an E.R. nurse, when her dreams of going to college to pursue that career had crumbled. It was Miss Joan who'd had faith in her when she had lost all of it herself. And Miss Joan had come through without a word of criticism or complaint when Holly suddenly found herself a mother—without the excitement of having gone the usual route to get to that state.

She flashed a smile at the woman now, tucked away her starry-eyed look and got back to work. Miss Joan wasn't paying her to daydream.

Chapter Two

"C'mon, Holly, say yes," Laurie Hodges, one of Miss Joan's part-time waitresses, coaxed as she followed Holly around the diner.

The latter was clearing away glasses and dishes bearing the remnants of customers' lunches.

Every so often Laurie would pick up a dish, too, and pile it onto her tray. But the twenty-four-year-old's mind wasn't on her work, it was on convincing her friend to do something else *besides* work.

"You never have any fun," Laurie complained, lowering her voice so that those who were still in the diner wouldn't overhear. Bending slightly so as to get a better look at Holly's face, she continued trying to chip away at Holly's resolve. "You want to look back twenty years from now, sitting alone in your house, watching shadows swallow each other up on the wall and lamenting that you never devoted any time to creating memories to look back on? For pity's sake, Holly, all you ever do is work." Laurie said it in an accusing voice, emphasizing the last part as if it was a curse word.

Well, she certainly couldn't argue with that, Holly

thought. But there was a very good reason for that. "That's because that's all there is."

At least, that was all there was in her world.

There was her job as a full-time waitress, and when her shift was over and Miss Joan didn't need her for any extra work, she went home, where an entirely different kind of work was waiting for her. The work that every woman did when she had a family and a home to look after.

In her case, she looked after her mother, whose range of activities was limited by her condition and the wheelchair that had all but kept her prisoner these past few years. She also took care of her niece, Molly, who at four, going all too quickly on five, was a handful and a half to keep up with.

Then, of course, there was the house, which didn't clean itself. And when all that was taken care of, she had the courses she was taking online. Granted, they were strategically arranged around her limited time, but they were still there, waiting for her to dive into and work through them.

All in all, that usually comprised a twenty-three-and-a-half-hour day.

That left a minimum of time to be used for such frivolous things like eating and sleeping, both of which she did on a very limited basis.

And *that,* in turn, left absolutely *no* time for things such as going out with friends and just doing nothing—or, as Laurie was proposing, going dancing at Murphy's.

"That is *not* all there is," Laurie argued with her. "My God, Holly, make some time for yourself before you're a shriveled up old prune living with nothing but a bunch of regrets."

Laurie caught Holly's arm to corner her attention when it seemed as if her words were just bouncing off Holly's head, unheard, unheeded. Holly was easygoing, but she didn't like being backed into a corner physically or verbally.

She raised her eyes. The deadly serious look in them caused Laurie to drop her hand. But she didn't stop talking.

"They're going to have an actual *band* that's going to be playing Friday night. One of the Murphy brothers and a couple of his friends," she elaborated. "Liam, I think." Laurie took a guess at which brother was playing. "Or maybe it's Finn. I just know it's not Brett." Brett was the eldest and ran the place. All three lived above the family-owned saloon. "But anyway, it doesn't matter which of the Murphy brothers it is, the point is that there's going to be live people playing music for the rest of us to dance to."

"Might be interesting if they were having dead people playing music," Miss Joan commented, coming up behind the two young women.

Rather than looking flustered and rushing away, pretending to look busy, Laurie brazenly appealed to the diner owner to back her up.

"Tell her, Miss Joan," Laurie entreated. "Tell this pig-headed woman that she only gets one chance at being young."

"Unlike the many chances I give you to actually act like a waitress," Miss Joan said, her eyes narrowing as she gave the fast-talking Laurie a scrutinizing look. "Don't you have sugar dispensers to fill?" It was a rhetorical question. One that had Laurie instantly backing away and running off to comply.

Once the other waitress had hurried away, Miss Joan turned her attention back to Holly. "She's right, you know," Miss Joan said, lowering her voice. "I hate to admit it, all things considered, but Laurie is right. You do only have one chance to be young. You can act like a fool kid in your sixties, like some of those pea-brained wranglers who come here to eat, but you and I know that the only right time to behave that way is when you *are* young. Like now," she told Holly pointedly. "Did Laurie have anything specific in mind? Or was she just rambling on the way she usually does? If that girl had a real thought in her head, it would die of loneliness," she declared, shaking her head.

"She had something specific in mind," Holly reluctantly told her.

Holly braced herself. She could already see whose side Miss Joan was on. She loved and respected the redheaded woman and she didn't want to be at odds with her, but she *really* had no time to waste on something as trivial as dancing, which she didn't do very well anyway. She just wished the whole subject would just fade away.

Miss Joan waited a second but Holly didn't say anything more. "Are you going to give me details, or am I supposed to guess what that 'specific' thing is?" Miss Joan asked.

Unable to pile any more dishes onto the tray, Holly hefted it and started across the diner. With Miss Joan eyeing every step she took, Holly had no choice but to tell her what she wanted to know.

Reluctantly, she recited the details Miss Joan asked for.

"There's a band playing at Murphy's this Friday. Laurie and some of her friends are planning to go there around nine to check it out. And to dance," she added.

Miss Joan nodded, taking it all in. "So why aren't you going?" she asked.

Holly shrugged carelessly. "I've got too much to do."

"Why aren't you going?" Miss Joan repeated, as if the excuse she'd just given the diner owner wasn't nearly good enough to be taken seriously. Before Holly could answer, the woman went on to recite all the reasons why she *should* go. "It's after your shift. I'm sure that your mother is capable enough to baby-sit Molly, especially since it'll be past your niece's bedtime—and if for some reason your mother can't, then honey, I certainly can."

That surprised Holly. She knew that Miss Joan tended to be less blustery with children, but that still didn't mean that she was a substitute Mary Poppins.

"You'd watch her?" Holly asked incredulously.

"Sure. I've got to get in more practice babysitting, seeing as how my first grandbaby is almost here," Miss Joan answered, referring to the baby that Alma, Ray's sister, and Cash, her stepson, were having. The baby was due at the beginning of January, and as time grew shorter, the woman was becoming increasingly excited.

"I couldn't ask you to do that," Holly protested. "Even on standby."

Miss Joan frowned at her. "Unless my hearing's

going, girl—and I'm pretty damn sure that it isn't, you *didn't* ask me to babysit this Friday night. I just offered." With her hands on her small hips Miss Joan fixed her with a penetrating look. "Okay, you got any other excuses you want shot down?"

Apparently Miss Joan was not about to take no for an answer. But Holly wasn't ready to capitulate just yet, either. "I've got classes."

Miss Joan made a dismissive noise. "*Online* classes," she emphasized with a small snort. "That means you can take them the next day. Or on Sunday, if you're busy making memories Saturday night." The final comment was punctuated with a lusty chuckle.

Holly blushed to the roots of her long, straight blond hair. "Miss Joan." The name was more of a plea than anything else. Though she knew Miss Joan didn't mean to, the woman was embarrassing her.

"Lots of ways to make memories," Miss Joan informed her, brushing aside the obvious meaning behind the previous phrase she'd used. She looked at Holly intently. "Okay, like I said, any other excuses?"

"Yes, a big one," Holly answered, unloading the last of the dishes onto the conveyor belt that would snake the dishes through the dishwashing machine against the far wall. "I really don't know how to dance." Because she felt it was a shortcoming, she said the words to the wall next to the conveyor belt, rather than to Miss Joan's face.

"Well, that's an easy one to fix," Miss Joan informed her, brushing the excuse aside as if it was an annoying gnat. "Dancing's fun. I can teach you. Or my husband, Harry, can. You want someone younger,

I'll ask Cash to show you the finer points," she said, waiting to hear who Holly wanted to go with.

Had Miss Joan forgotten that her stepson was in a very unique situation? "Just what he wants to be doing when his wife's on the verge of having their first baby. Teaching me how to dance," Holly quipped.

"Sure, why not?" Miss Joan asked. "I think it's perfect. It'll take his mind off worrying about everything for a little while—and it'll perform a useful service for you."

Holly sighed. The woman was like a Hydra monster. No matter how many heads she lopped off, Miss Joan just grew some more and kept coming right back at her.

"Miss Joan, I appreciate everything you're trying to do here, I really do," Holly said emphatically. "But I don't have time for any dancing lessons, just like I don't have time to go to Murphy's and—"

Out of the blue, Miss Joan gave her a look. The kind of look that made strong men doubt the validity of their cause and rendered frightened young waitresses like Laurie speechless. Holly, however, was made of far sterner stuff than the average person, due to all the responsibility she had shouldered from a very young age.

So she braced herself and listened, hoping she could offer a successful rebuttal.

"You like working here at the diner, girl?" Miss Joan finally asked after a sufficient amount of time had gone by.

Here it comes, Holly thought. "Yes, ma'am, you know that I do."

Miss Joan's expressive eyes narrowed, bringing

in her penciled-in eyebrows. "Then if you want to have a job on Monday, you'll go to Murphy's with your friends on Friday *and you will have fun*," she ordered forcefully.

"Hey, old woman." Eduardo, the longtime cook, called to her as he stopped puttering around in his kitchen and came forward. "You cannot just order someone to have fun. It does not work that way, but then, perhaps you have never had any fun yourself so you would not know that."

"Maybe *you* can't order someone to have fun, but *I* can," Miss Joan assured the short-order cook in a voice that said she wasn't going to brook any sort of rebellion or challenge, especially from him.

That resolved, Miss Joan turned her attention back to Holly. "So, girl, what'll it be? You going to Murphy's on Friday night and coming to work on Monday, or are you staying home, studying and looking for a new job come Monday morning?" Miss Joan asked.

"You wouldn't fire me over something like that," Holly pointed out with some certainty.

"No," Miss Joan agreed and let her savor that for approximately two seconds before adding, "I'd fire you over your insubordination." When Holly looked at her, confusion in her eyes, Miss Joan elaborated. "I told you to do something and you out-and-out refused. That's pretty sassy if you ask me." Miss Joan smiled at her, and it was one of the few genuine smiles that seemed to register on the woman's lips and in her hazel eyes, as well. "In other words, insubordination. So what'll it be?" she prodded, waiting to hear the answer she *wanted* to hear.

Holly sighed. She'd known in her heart it was going to end this way.

"I'll go," she said.

Miss Joan's eyes met hers and it almost felt as if the woman was delving into her very soul as she asked in a clear voice, "You're sure?"

"Yes, ma'am, I'm sure. I'll go," Holly repeated, still not certain how this had all come about now that she looked back at it. "But I won't dance." That, to her, was as far as she was willing to concede. She absolutely refused to make a complete fool of herself.

At least she would be among friends, she consoled herself.

For the time being, what Miss Joan had heard seemed to be enough, though she shook her head as if despairing over the young woman. "I guess you can lead the filly to the dance floor, but you can't make her dance. Still, something is better than nothing, I always say." She patted Holly's shoulder. "Good girl. Remember to have fun. That's an order," she added with a near growl.

"What did she say?" Laurie asked, venturing forward rather quickly once Miss Joan had made her way to the opposite end of the diner. Laurie looked as if she was dying of curiosity.

Holly began putting down fresh place settings at each table that was no longer occupied. Rather than helping, Laurie just started to follow her around again, oblivious to her obligations as a waitress who was *not* on a break.

"She told me to go out with you, Cyndy and Reta on Friday," Holly told her.

Laurie's eyes all but lit up. They were definitely

wider. "Really? How about that? There's hope for the old girl yet." Laurie laughed, glancing over her shoulder to where Miss Joan was behind the counter. And then she turned her attention back to Holly. "So you gonna listen?"

Holly was fairly certain that Miss Joan wouldn't fire her over something as trivial as this, but if she were honest with herself, she wasn't a hundred percent sure. Miss Joan had been known to do some very strange things in her time, all because she felt she was right. The very last thing Holly wanted was to challenge the woman.

Besides, on the outside chance that Miss Joan had meant what she said, she definitely couldn't afford to lose her job. Granted, there were other jobs in Forever, but she had gotten comfortable in this one. There was the added fact that Miss Joan allowed her to take leftovers home to her mother and Molly.

It might not seem like a lot to someone else, but she was of a mind that every tiny bit helped. Someday, when she finally got her nursing degree and her courage up to ask Dr. Davenport if he'd hire her as his nurse, she intended to pay Miss Joan back for all the times the older woman had looked the other way and allowed her to bend the rules.

Like the time that her mother and Molly were both sick and she had to stay home to take care of them. Miss Joan not only allowed her to take the two days off, but she paid her for them as if she was at work. And, on top of that, she'd sent over one of the waitresses with soup for her mother and niece, and food for her because, "If I know her, that fool girl will be so busy taking care of her family, she'll forget to eat herself."

Miss Joan had been right, Holly recalled. She *had* been so busy caring for the two patients she'd entirely forgotten to eat.

Miss Joan always covered all the bases, Holly thought with no small amount of affection.

Her eyes dancing, it was obvious to Holly that Laurie was making even *more* plans for Friday night. The young waitress looked as if she was ready to go now rather than have to wait until the end of the week.

"If you don't have anything to wear," Laurie suddenly said, turning toward her, "you can borrow something from my closet. We're about the same size," she guesstimated, looking Holly up and down. "I'll be happy to share anything I've got."

Did Laurie think that she was *that* poor? "I've got a dress," Holly protested with a touch of indignation she didn't bother hiding.

"Oh." Holly's response had clearly surprised her. "Okay, then you're all set," she said happily. "I'll come by to pick you up at 7:30 p.m. Friday night."

She didn't want Laurie going out of her way. "Why don't I just meet you there?" Holly suggested.

"Because you won't," Laurie responded. She looked at her friend. "I know you, Holly, so don't even go there. I'll pick you up," she repeated. "And we'll have fun," she promised with feeling. "You'll see."

With all the things she had on her mind, Holly thought, she highly doubted it. But she knew better than to say so.

So instead, she forced a quick flash of a smile to

her lips, then murmured something about having "inventory to do" as she walked away from Laurie and headed toward the tiny back office.

Chapter Three

Her time factor down to the wire, Holly stared into the small, narrow closet in her bedroom. She'd been staring into it for a couple of minutes now.

It wasn't as if she was trying to decide what to wear, because there was so much to choose from. There wasn't. She knew every article of clothing that hung there by heart.

She had exactly one all-purpose dress that she'd worn to her high school graduation, to the funeral of a friend of her mother's and to a small number of other, lesser occasions. Money was tight. She saw no reason to spend it on something frivolous when there were so many more worthy items that needed to be bought first—like toys that lit up Molly's eyes and clothes for the girl's ever-growing little body.

The all-purpose, A-line, navy blue dress was certainly still in decent condition, but she had to secretly admit that part of her wished she'd taken Laurie up on her offer when the waitress had suggested lending her a dress for this evening.

The next moment, Holly shrugged the thought away. Murphy's wasn't all that well lit anyway, and besides, she was not looking to impress anyone. She was just giving in and going out tonight so that Laurie and Miss Joan would stop saying she needed to get out more and socialize.

After all, it wasn't as if she was bored. God knew she had more than enough to keep her busy, and she didn't feel a lack of anything in her life. She wasn't looking for a boyfriend or a husband. Her heart definitely wasn't up for grabs.

It was already spoken for.

She'd been in love with Ray for as long as she could remember. That wasn't going to change, and as long as she felt that way, she wasn't about to go looking for a boyfriend. She wouldn't feel right about it. Her heart definitely wouldn't be in it.

She'd never been one of those girls who felt she needed a man at her side to complete her. She knew better than that. She had always been her own person, and that person was as busy as any two or three people had a right to be.

"You know, it doesn't matter how long you stare into it, nothing new is going to pop up in that closet," Martha Johnson said as she wheeled herself into her daughter's small, tidy bedroom.

"I know, Mom," Holly acknowledged wearily, still staring into her closet. "I was just wondering if it wouldn't be better all around if I just stayed home tonight." She certainly didn't need to dig for excuses. She had plenty of those. "I've got that test to study for and Molly's just getting over a cold—"

"At this age, Molly's *always* going to be getting over a cold," Martha pointed out patiently. "And from what I understand, the beauty of taking those courses in the isolating privacy of your own room is that you can take those tests whenever you want—on your own schedule, not the teacher's or whoever it is that's hiding on the other side of that monitor. Anyway, you're going and that's that."

"Mom, what if Molly wakes up—" She got no further. Her mother had raised her hand, calling for silence.

"So she wakes up. I'll handle it. Don't make me feel any more of an invalid than this chair already makes me feel, Holly," she pleaded. "Besides, you wouldn't want this dress to go to waste, would you?"

"What dress?" Holly asked, finally turning around to look at her mother.

That was when she saw it. What her mother was talking about. There on her lap, encased in a plastic, see-through garment bag, was a dress that gave new meaning to the word *beautiful*.

Holly's mouth dropped open in complete awe—and concern. The dress *had* to be expensive. She wasn't about to allow her mother to throw away money on her like that, especially since there wasn't all that much to toss around. They were still paying off the medical bills associated with the car accident that had put her mother into that wheelchair.

"Mom, you didn't—"

"No, Holly, I didn't," Martha quickly assured her daughter.

Her mother didn't usually lie to her, yet there was the dress, on her lap. "Then where did that come from?" Holly asked.

Martha Johnson smiled. "Miss Joan's husband, Harry, brought it over. He said she told him that this was for you and that you weren't allowed to give it back or refuse it, otherwise you're out of a job," her mother said matter-of-factly. She looked down at the dress that was still on her lap. "If you ask me, this'll look extremely pretty on you." And then she looked up to see Holly's reaction.

That was *not* the expression of a woman who was thrilled about getting a new dress.

Holly was frowning.

"Oh, Holly, smile. You look as if you are about to be sent to prison, not to enjoy a rare night out. A *well-deserved* night out, I might add," Martha insisted. She shook her head, her salt-and-pepper hair moving back and forth from the motion. "Honey, I can't remember the last time you went out for fun."

Neither could she, actually, Holly thought. But that still didn't make this any easier for her. Holly bit her lower lip. "Mom, I won't fit in."

"You won't fit in if you wear that old navy blue dress of yours," Martha pointed out, nodding at the dress that was still hanging in the closet. "In this bright, pretty little thing, you'll still stand out," she acknowledged, nodding at the glittery blue-gray dress, "but in a good way. Besides, you're going out with your friends, aren't you? That should make it easier for you."

She really wasn't all that close to the girls she was going out with. Not so much that she could really call them her friends.

Holly raised one shoulder in a helpless gesture. "I'm going out with girls I work with, Mom."

"Close enough," her mother pronounced.

There was no doubt about it, Holly thought. She was going to feel awkward. She had trouble blending in in situations outside of her comfort zone, at work or home. Anything beyond that was no longer in her zone.

Martha took her hand between both of hers, a sympathetic look in her eyes. "Honey, the more you hide, the harder it's going to be on you to come out and mingle with people who aren't sitting at the counter, giving you their lunch orders." If Holly could be outgoing in that situation—which she was—then she had it in her to be outgoing in other kinds of situations. She just had to be drawn out. "My friends occasionally drop by the diner and they all tell me that you're the nicest, most helpful girl there—"

"Yes, but that's work," Holly reminded her. And that was exactly her point. She was fine as long as she could hide behind her job. No one expected any real one-on-one time with her while she was at work.

Martha was not about to accept defeat. In her own way, she was as stubborn as her daughter. "Then pretend you're at work tonight—just don't go behind the bar and start serving drinks," Martha warned with an understanding smile.

"Mom, I—" The doorbell rang, interrupting what she was going to say next. Her head swung in the direction of the front door. "Oh, God, that's Laurie." She glanced toward her mother. "She said she was going to swing by to pick me up because she didn't trust me to come to Murphy's on my own."

Martha looked just the slightest bit impressed, as well as surprised. "That Laurie is smarter than she looks." Maneuvering her wheelchair so that she was closer to her daughter's double bed, Martha deposited the new dress on it, then announced, "You get ready. I'll let Laurie in and tell her that you'll need a few extra minutes. She'll understand."

Holly's stomach officially tied itself up in a knot. The kind that threatened to cut off her air supply. She pressed her hand against her stomach. "Tell her I'm sick."

"Holly Ann Johnson, you know how I feel about lying," Martha informed her, pretending to look stern.

"But I think I am coming down with something," Holly protested. "I feel feverish."

Martha frowned, wheeling herself over to her daughter. "Bend down," she ordered.

Holly had no idea what her mother was up to. "Mom, I—"

"I said bend down," Martha repeated even as the doorbell pealed again. When Holly did as she was instructed, her mother leaned forward in her chair and employed the classic mother's thermometer: she brushed her lips lightly across her daughter's forehead. "Cool as a cucumber," she pronounced, motioning for her to straighten up again. "No fever present." Her eyes narrowed. "You're going. No argument."

With that, Martha wheeled herself out of the room as the doorbell rang a third time.

Holly sighed. Okay, she silently argued with herself, searching for the pros in this. After all, how humiliating could this be? She was going out with a bunch of girls from the diner, and while they weren't bosom buddies, she did know them, at least to varying degrees. They'd go to Murphy's, have a couple of beers—or, in her case, a single sangria—eat a few oversalted peanuts and listen to this band that Laurie had gone on about for the past two days.

If guys came by and asked the other girls to dance, leaving her alone at the bar, she knew Brett Murphy—the bartender who was most likely on duty tonight—well enough to have a conversation with him while she waited for her friends to come back.

She didn't consider what she'd do if someone asked her to dance, because she was more than fairly certain that no one would. As far as she was concerned, she didn't think of herself as the type to attract the attention of anybody, except maybe someone who desperately didn't want to leave alone at closing time. And when it came to fending off someone like that, well, she could handle herself in those sorts of situations. Just before he'd left home, Will had gotten interested in martial arts and he'd taught her a few self-defense moves that would come in handy in dicey situations.

Okay, enough thinking, time for dressing, she silently ordered herself.

Hurrying into the blue-gray dress, she had to admit she liked the feel of the material as it glided passed her hips, stopping several inches above her knee—quite a bit shorter than the navy dress.

She wasn't accustomed to wearing anything this short—or this clingy, she thought, looking herself over in the narrow full-length mirror that hung on the back of her door.

The fabric looked almost shimmery, she thought, staring at her image as she turned first in one direction then the other.

Holly didn't realize she was smiling until she caught her reflection.

Running a comb through her hair, she decided to leave it down. After all, she wasn't trying to attract any undue attention, and the dress looked as if it could do more than that on its own.

For a second, she debated taking it off again and slipping on her faithful old navy dress, but she had a strong suspicion that Miss Joan had eyes everywhere, and if she wore her navy dress to Murphy's, Miss Joan would know and get on her case about that.

Besides, this had to have cost the woman a pretty penny, she thought as she lovingly glided her hand along her hip.

Holly took a deep breath. "Okay, ready or not, here I come."

Grabbing her hoop earrings from the top of her bureau—a gift from her mother on her graduation day—she put them on as she walked toward the front of the house. The earrings were the one good piece of jewelry she had besides the small gold cross her father had given her on the first day of school.

She heard voices coming from the living room.

As she drew closer, Holly cocked her head, listening intently.

She could make out her mother's voice, but the voice that was answering her mother didn't sound anything like Laurie—or any other female she knew, except possibly Miss Joan. But even Miss Joan's voice wasn't this deep.

If she didn't know any better, she would have said that the voice she heard belonged to—

Holly's heart began to pound the way it always did whenever she first heard his voice and realized he was somewhere close by.

"Ray?" she asked as she walked into the small living room.

Ray shifted his brown eyes toward her a beat after he uttered a preoccupied, "Hi." But once he actually focused on her, the greeting was immediately followed by an awestruck, "Wow," and then a joking request for some sort of proof of identity.

"Doll, is that really you?" Ray asked, staring at her and cocking his head as if that could somehow help him clear his vision, or at least allow him to make a better identification of the shimmering fairy princess entering the room. He took a step toward her, staring so hard his eyes all but burned into her. "Wow," he said again. "You clean up really well," he told her, appreciation all but vibrating in his voice.

"Doesn't she, though?" Martha said, pride brimming over in her voice as she, too, turned around to face Holly.

A warm, pleased feeling swept through her, but she told herself that Ray was just being nice. After all, they were friends and they'd known each other since they were children.

"What are you doing here?" she asked him. Holly glanced around, expecting to see Laurie somewhere in the room, but there was no indication that he'd come with anyone.

What was going on here?

"Well, this afternoon I happened to mention to Laurie's brother that I was going to see if Liam could play half as well as he thinks he can, and I guess Laurie overheard me because next thing I know, she's asking me for a favor, saying that she and her friends were going to Murphy's tonight, too. Her problem was that she didn't have enough room in her car for everyone. She thought that since you and I are friends, maybe I wouldn't mind picking you up and taking you with me." He shrugged casually. "I said sure, why not. Why didn't you tell me you were going tonight?" he asked. "You know that I would have taken you—like I am now."

Her shrug matched his, except that hers was tinged with self-consciousness. "It kind of just came up as a spur-of-the-moment, last-minute thing," she told him, deliberately avoiding his gaze.

His eyes swept over her as the corners of his mouth curved in a smile that could only be described as wicked.

"That dress certainly doesn't look like a spur-of-the-moment thing," he told her.

In all the time that he'd known Holly, he'd never seen her looking this good, this, well, sexy for lack of a better word. Did she even know that? That she looked really hot? He had a feeling that, this being Holly, she didn't.

He had a full agenda planned for tonight, but it looked as if he might have to add chaperone to that list. As her friend, he didn't want to see guys hit on her if that made her uncomfortable.

Seeing that Holly was momentarily stuck for a response to Ray's assessment of the dress that adorned her body, Martha came to her daughter's rescue.

"That was a birthday present I gave her last year. You know how Holly is, she saves things until the very last minute—even leaves the tags on until she wears the item for the first time," she added, seeing that there was one telltale tag hanging from the back of the stunning dress. Shifting her wheelchair so that she was behind her daughter, Martha drew close enough to remove the tag with one well-executed yank.

"I knew it would look good on you," she told her daughter, playing her part to the hilt.

"Good?" Ray echoed incredulously. "Doll, you're downright beautiful in that."

"She's downright beautiful without it, too," Martha told him. The way she saw it, Holly enhanced the clothing she wore, not the other way around.

"Mom!" Holly cried, mortified at the implication of the words.

"No, she's right," Ray cut in. "You're a beautiful person, especially on the inside, Doll. I've always said that." He had a feeling it was getting late. "Okay, you ready to go?" he asked, glancing at his watch. He'd expected to be there by now, looking over the crop of women the band had attracted. "The first set is at eight and I want to get there before that, look over the crowd and all that good stuff," he told her.

She felt her heart go back to its regular measured beat. She knew what he meant by "good stuff." How could she forget? If Ray was going to Murphy's, it was because he wanted to see if the promise of a band had drawn any new faces from the neighboring towns and places farther south.

"Well, we wouldn't want you to be late," she told him glibly.

"You two have fun, now," Martha told them as she followed in their wake to the front door. "Don't worry about Molly—or anything else, either," she instructed Holly. "Just for one night, please act your age and not mine."

"Good advice, Mrs. Johnson. I'll see that she follows it," Ray promised the woman with a bright smile. "Okay, milady, your chariot awaits," he told Holly grandly, bowing from the waist and gesturing toward the truck that he always drove.

"I see that your 'chariot's' been freshly washed," she teased as she opened the passenger-side door and got in.

"Can't make a good impression in a dirty chariot, now, can I?" he asked with a laugh, getting in on his side.

Holly made no reply.

She knew that the good impression he was talking about referred to whatever woman he set his sights on tonight, but just for the moment, she pretended that he'd actually done this for her and that he was her date, not just a friend doing another friend a favor.

Chapter Four

"Seriously, Doll," Ray said to her as he pulled away from the single-story house she called home. "You could have given me a call, told me you wanted to go hear Liam play tonight. I would have been more than happy to swing by and pick you up."

He eased his foot off the gas pedal of his Super Duty pickup truck and glanced in Holly's direction.

Damn, but she looked different tonight. He'd been spending too much time looking *through* her that he hadn't realized just how really pretty his best friend was.

Really pretty.

He found it difficult to pull his eyes away.

When she made no answer to his comment, Ray went on talking. "Don't mind saying that I was kind of surprised when I heard that you were actually stepping out for a change."

He flashed Holly a wide grin, the one that the girls he'd been out with referred to as his *killer* grin, except that with Holly, he wasn't trying to prove anything or charm her the way he did when he was out on a date. Since this was Holly, the grin he flashed at her was completely genuine.

"Good for you," he congratulated her heartily, still on the subject of her finally stepping out on Friday night. "I guess you're really not the stick-in-the-mud that you pretend to be."

Holly squared her shoulders, taking offense at the careless assessment he'd just tossed at her. "First, I don't 'pretend' to be anything—I never do. And second, I am *not,* nor have I ever been, a stick-in-the-mud, Ray Rodriguez," she retorted with feeling.

"Okay," Ray allowed expansively. "Exactly what would *you* call doing nothing but working 24/7?" he asked.

Holly sniffed as she lifted her chin defensively. "Being responsible."

"A responsible stick-in-the-mud," he qualified, underscoring the descriptive phrase he'd just used. Then, seeing that his teasing was apparently getting under Holly's skin, he shrugged, dismissing the semantics they were butting heads over. "Hey, it's just good to see you going out, Doll." He inclined his head in her direction, as if that would help him hear her response better as he drove. "Got your sights set on anybody in particular?" he asked curiously.

Yes, the lunkhead sitting next to me. "Nobody," she told him firmly. "I just want to hear the band play, see if they're any good."

Since this was Holly and they told each other everything—even though the dress she had on clearly negated the seemingly innocent reason behind her going out tonight—he took her at her word.

"Well, Liam's brothers seem to think so," Ray told her. "They think he's got real potential. Brett even had a small area cleared off to serve as a dance floor.

The way I see it, the music has to be good in order for people to dance."

She smiled, thinking of something Laurie had said to her about the band. "Not really," she interjected. "It just has to be good and loud."

He laughed, remembering what he'd overheard her friend saying as he talked to Laurie's brother. "Laurie just wants to give Neil Parsons an excuse to put his arms around her," Ray said.

"Neil Parsons?" Holly echoed. "Are you sure?"

This was the first she'd heard anything about Laurie wanting to get close to Neil. When Laurie had talked to her about coming tonight, she'd made it sound as if she was trying to talk her into a girls' night out, an occasion where they and a couple of the other girls who worked at Miss Joan's diner would get loud and just have some fun listening to Liam trying to hit all the right notes. Laurie hadn't said a word about wanting to get close to Neil.

Deliberately?

"I'm sure," Ray said casually, completely ignorant of the way what he'd just said had thrown Holly for a loop. "That's what she told her brother. She also said that Cyndy Adams was hoping to catch Ty Smith's eye, as well. Come to think of it, Laurie mentioned Reta Wells, too, but I didn't hear the name of the guy that Reta was looking to corner."

"So they're all looking to get partnered up?" Holly asked.

She was doing her best to hide the distressed feeling that was growing in the pit of her stomach. Why hadn't Laurie leveled with her?

Because she knew you'd never agree to come if she

mentioned being interested in catching some guy's eye. You know that.

"It sounded like that to me," Ray told her. And then he shrugged. "But, hey, I could be wrong. And even if I'm right, this just might be a fishing expedition on their parts. I think that if this was a done deal, they would have all gotten paired off before they ever got to Murphy's. So, if this is just in the works, it's all going to be casual," he assured her. Ray slanted a look in her direction. "You *sure* there's nobody you're looking to cut out of the herd?" he asked her.

"I'm sure," she answered firmly. She'd *known* this was a bad idea. Holly glanced over her shoulder at the road they'd just traveled. "Look, maybe you'd better take me back home."

Ray just kept driving the way he'd been going, heading toward Murphy's.

"Sorry, Doll, I told you I don't want to be late for Liam's first number. I'm *really* curious to see how he does. Besides, if I take you back now, that knock-'em-dead dress'll go to waste, since I'd be the only one who's seen it on you," he maintained.

You're the only one who counts.

Why did he have to be so thickheaded when it came to this? Holly wondered in frustration.

Out loud she merely said, "I can always save it for another time."

"C'mon, Doll, where's your sense of adventure? Let your hair down," he prompted.

"Maybe you need an eye exam," she told him with a touch of sarcasm. "My hair *is* down."

"See?" he asked with that same disarming grin. "Halfway there."

Holly sighed and, for the moment, gave up as she slouched back in her seat.

The trip was all but over.

Murphy's looked as if it had been infused with a community of fireflies; it was so lit up that it was visible from a few blocks away.

"I guess word must have gotten around about Liam and his band," she speculated.

Ray laughed. "He'd better be good. If he's not, he's going to fall flat on his face in front of a packed house."

She caught herself having performance jitters for the middle Murphy brother. "I think they're probably more than ready to meet him halfway," she said. At least she hoped so, for the sake of Liam's pride.

Everyone in Forever knew everyone else. That meant that, by and large, they pretty much had each others' backs. While some occasional petty jealousies might surface between the inhabitants of Forever and the people who lived on the surrounding ranches, for the most part, everyone wished everyone else well.

Ray pulled up in front of the saloon. Then, seeing that there was no space to park his truck, he circled around to a larger lot in the back. Usually there were plenty of spaces to be had there. Tonight Ray found that he had to drive up one lane and down another before he finally found a space where he could park his truck. He pulled it in between two 4x4s of almost identical color—battleship gray.

"Sure hope this means he's selling beer to all these car owners," he commented, looking around the lot.

The offhanded comment caught her attention. She

looked at Ray sharply. "Why? Is Brett having trouble staying in the black?"

Brett Murphy wasn't the kind who talked about money problems except in the most casual way, making it sound as if there was no problem at all.

"Mike heard him say something about having a note come due on Murphy's next month," Ray answered.

He and his siblings certainly knew what it was like to have their backs up against a wall and the bank breathing down their necks, Ray thought. They'd almost lost the ranch after their mother had died. Pulling together as a family had been the only thing that had saved them from foreclosure. Even though he was the youngest, the experience had made him hypersensitive to other people's problems when it came to needing money for payments due.

"I think that's the reason behind Brett agreeing to have Liam get his friends together and play tonight. Having a packed house never hurts," Ray told her as he pocketed the keys to his truck.

Holly looked out at all the cars parked outside the saloon. It looked as if everyone in town had shown up, not to mention that there appeared to be vehicles from some of the neighboring towns, as well.

"Well, whatever his reason, I think he's going to be up all night counting the saloon's take from tonight," Holly predicted.

They could hear the noise coming from the saloon even inside the cab of the truck. She estimated that it would be close to deafening once they were inside the small, rectangular building that was both the place of business for the three Murphy brothers and their home since they lived right above the saloon. "Maybe we should have brought earplugs," she all but shouted to Ray.

She saw him grinning at her. It was the kind of grin that acknowledged he was aware she'd said something to him, but hadn't a clue what that something had been.

It didn't matter to her if Ray had heard her or not; the important thing was being this close to him. She hadn't seen him for the past couple of days and had assumed that work on the ranch was keeping him busy.

Either that, or a new love interest had come into his life. That happened with a fair amount of regularity— like clockwork.

Holly shut down the idea as soon as it occurred to her, preferring not to think about it.

But since Ray hadn't mentioned anyone's name on the way over here—and he would have had there been someone new—she just assumed that tonight he'd be back on the prowl again. One of his brothers— Mike—had made the observation that Ray changed girlfriends the way other men changed undershirts while working out in the hot sun.

What that meant to her was that Ray wasn't getting serious about any of the women he went out with— which was just the way she liked it.

Someday, Holly firmly hoped, Ray Rodriguez would come to his senses and realize that what he had been looking for all this time had been standing right there in front of him all along. The fact that he'd said more than once that he wasn't looking for that special someone didn't carry any weight with her. It was a rare man who admitted that he wanted a wife in his life, that he wanted something other than to be a carefree, love-'em-and-leave-'em man that all the available women in the area—and some who weren't so available—flocked to.

Just before he opened the front door to Murphy's, Ray bent close to her ear and promised, "Don't worry. I won't leave you until we find Laurie."

The moment he said that, Holly fervently hoped that Laurie and her friends had gotten stuck in some parallel universe and had, for all intents and purposes, disappeared off the face of the earth for the duration of the evening.

Her wish to that end intensified when, to her surprise, Ray took her hand. "So we don't get separated," he explained.

The explanation came with an accompanying puff of warm breath—his—that instantly seemed to sink right into the sensitive skin along her neck and cheek.

For a split second, Holly thought her heart was going to burst through her chest, it was hammering that hard. But she managed to take in, hold and then release two long, even breaths, which in turn steadied her pulse—or got it as steady as was humanly possible, given the circumstances.

She took another long breath before saying, "I'm not worried."

He turned to look at her over his shoulder, guessing she'd said something but the din from the saloon had completely swallowed it up.

"What?" he asked, his voice just a decibel below shouting.

This time, it was her turn to lean forward and bring

her lips to his ear. "I said, I'm not worried," she repeated.

Something tightened in his gut as he felt her breath
along his ear. It sent a reflexive shiver through a large
part of him, which surprised him. Feeling slightly un-
settled, his eyes met hers.

And held.

For just an isolated fragment of time, Ray felt
something happening, although what that *something*
was, he wasn't sure. He just knew it was something.
Something unusual.

Something different.

The next moment it was gone.

Whether he'd shaken it off or it had just been ab-
sorbed by the noise and the atmosphere, he didn't
know. All he knew was that it was gone. And he was
relieved.

And maybe just a little saddened, as well.

Turning from her, feeling just the slightest bit un-
steady on his feet—as if he'd just gotten up from his
sickbed to come here—Ray carefully scanned the
crowd directly in front of him.

The band, he could see, was just setting up. Which
meant that he and Holly weren't late.

Instead of dwelling on the odd sensation in the
pit of his stomach, he focused on being able to hear
Liam's best efforts and on finding Holly's friends.
He knew he wouldn't feel right about just leaving
her alone here. It would be a little like abandoning
a newborn on the steps of a church in the middle of
the night. There was no telling if she'd be all right or
not until her friends found her.

He couldn't very well take Holly with him, though.

She was his best friend, but it somehow just didn't seem right to have her standing within earshot as he made his play for whatever female caught his fancy tonight. He could talk to Holly about it later—sans some of the more private details—but he didn't feel right having her actually witnessing him in action.

Not that he could really explain why; it just didn't feel right to him.

"Hey, there she is!" he cried out to Holly, spotting Laurie.

Since he was facing away from her, none of his words found her.

"What?" Holly raised her voice so that he could hear her, although their previous mode of exchange—through close proximity and long, warm glances, had clearly won her favor.

Turning to face her so that she could see his lips when he spoke, Ray repeated, "I found Laurie and the others."

"Great," Holly said, pasting a grateful smile she didn't feel on her lips as she said it.

All good things had to come to an end, she thought. She's always known that, she'd just been hoping that in this case, the end would take a little longer getting there. But then, she reminded herself, she hadn't been planning on coming out in the first place, so that any time she spent with Ray was actually a bonus.

Ray took her hand again and forged a path through the milling bodies of people she knew either by sight or by name. But she really wasn't focused on them— or on Laurie, either. Right now, all that mattered was that Ray was holding her hand.

And then he wasn't.

He'd dropped it, and the next moment she realized why. Laurie, Cyndy and Reta were right in front of her.

"Okay," Ray was saying to her, "Have a good time. That's an order, hear?"

She nodded her head. "I hear," she replied with another fake smile.

The next second, he was plowing his way through the crowd.

And then he was gone.

"Can't believe you actually made it," Laurie was saying enthusiastically, hooking her arm through Holly's. "We've got a table right over there." She pointed toward something in the distance, although she could have been pointing to a kangaroo for all the difference it made to Holly. "You can leave your coat and purse there," Laurie coaxed, drawing her to the table. "So that you can mingle better when the time comes."

She had no intension of mingling, better or otherwise, but to say so at this early stage was just looking for an argument. So instead, she made her way over to the table Laurie had indicated.

Once she reached the table, Holly shrugged off her coat and left it on the back of a chair. Her small purse she took with her. Who knew when she might need what was inside the small purse?

Turning to face Laurie, she saw a look of absolute wonder and appreciation in the other woman's soft brown eyes.

"Wow, no wonder you didn't want me to lend you one of my dresses." Her smile broadened. "You've been holding out on me, Holly."

Holly had no idea what the other woman was talking about. "Holding out?"

Laurie nodded, indicating the dress she had on. "I wouldn't have thought you owned something that special looking. You really do look sensational," she told Holly with the enthusiasm of a true friend. There wasn't so much as a note of jealousy in her voice. "You're definitely not going to have any trouble attracting attention from the testosterone set."

Red flags instantly went up all over the place in Holly's head. This was *not* going to be the uncomplicated evening that she'd hoped it would be.

"I don't want to attract any attention," Holly insisted, all but shouting the words into Laurie's ear. "I just came out tonight to hear the music."

And because you were going to nag me until I said yes, she added silently.

"That's not all you came for. Not in *that* dress," Laurie told her knowingly, saying the words directly into her ear so as to be heard.

There was no warm shiver going through her system the way there had been when Ray had talked to her. Instead, she could feel her stomach twisting for another reason.

She definitely shouldn't have given in and come here tonight. She was just leaving herself open to problems, problems she had neither the time nor the patience for.

The good part was over, Holly thought with a sinking feeling.

Chapter Five

"Look." Holly measured out her words slowly, trying to sound as calm as she could while having to practically shout at Laurie in order to be heard, even at this close proximity, "I don't want to be set up or pushed into anyone's arms. All I wanted when I said yes to you about going out was just a simple girls' night out, nothing else."

Struggling to hang on to her patience—and her bravado—Holly looked at the other waitress to see if she was getting through to her—or if Laurie had even actually heard her.

Laurie had obviously heard because she shouted back with a delighted smile, "We don't always get what we want, Holly."

I already knew that, Holly thought as she attempted not to let her thoughts show on her face even as she zeroed in on Ray. From what she could see, since he was halfway across the crowded floor, Ray looked as if he was talking up Emma Cross. Apparently, if that expression on Emma's face was any indication, he didn't have to do that much talking, either.

A sinking sensation was taking hold of her stomach again. This time it was more personal. She'd seen

Ray in action before, when they were in high school together, but it had been a while since she'd been a witness to the moves he could put on a girl when he was drawn to her.

Jealousy began to nibble away at the sedate exterior she was trying to project.

It hurt to watch, so she looked away.

She realized that Laurie was trying to ask her a question. Holly focused on her friend's mouth and finally heard what she was asking.

"What's your pleasure?" Laurie asked.

To go home, Holly thought but out loud she said, "Something simple. Vodka and orange juice, heavy on the orange juice."

"Naturally." The smile on Laurie's lips looked almost *too* accommodating.

Holly had a feeling that if the drink she'd just requested was going to be heavy on anything, it would be the vodka. Which was the *last* thing she needed at a time like this. Inebriated people did stupid things, and she prided herself on being in control. She intended for that to remain the case.

"Tell you what," Holly said, rising from the table, "I'll get my own drink. Be right back," she promised just before she started to make her way up to the bar.

She could feel the music throbbing in her chest, and the ever-increasing din of voices was already beginning to give her a headache. This was *not* promising, she thought darkly as she squeezed into the miniscule space that was available at the bar.

"What'll you have, beautiful?" Brett asked her.

The eldest Murphy brother seemed to materialize out of thin air. She could have sworn that he'd been on the far end of the bar as she'd begun her pilgrimage to the counter.

Beautiful, huh? The saloon owner obviously didn't recognize her, she decided. "Brett, it's me. Holly Johnson."

"I know who you are," he answered, a smile in his dark blue eyes as they met hers. "And you really do look beautiful," he told her, glancing at her dress. A sexy smile curved the corners of his mouth as he gave her a small piece of advice. "You've got to learn how to relax and take a compliment once in a while, Holly. That's the easy stuff. The hard stuff comes later," he said with a wink. "Now, what'll it be?"

What hard stuff? she couldn't help wondering. But out loud she answered his question. "Vodka and orange juice—heavy on the orange juice," she added.

If she'd been expecting an argument—or a joke—neither happened. Instead, Brett replied, "Coming right up," seamlessly capturing two different bottles and preparing the drink that she'd ordered.

Holly opened the small purse she'd brought with her—a purse that had practically no room for her wallet—when Brett placed the drink on the bar directly in front of her.

"How much do I owe you?" Holly asked, taking several bills out.

Brett shook his head. Picking up a dish towel, he wiped a spot up from the counter. "Beautiful women get the first drink of the evening on the house," he answered with a wink.

It'd been a while since she'd even had a drink. Holly had no idea how much she could safely imbibe, so she'd already made up her mind as to how much she was going to consume.

"I'm only getting the one," she told him.

Brett's smile never faded. "Then this won't be an expensive evening for you," he predicted.

And with that, he went down the bar as someone held up a glass.

Picking up the screwdriver Brett had made for her, Holly wove her way back to the table where she'd left her coat and Laurie.

But when she got there, Laurie was nowhere in sight. However, there was no empty place to mark her absence, and the chair that she had left her coat on before going to fetch her drink had somebody else sitting in it.

There were two guys she vaguely recognized sitting at the table, talking to Cyndy and Reta. Judging the expressions on the women's faces, these were the guys they had been looking to get together with tonight.

Laurie was probably with the guy she was interested in, as well. Dancing most likely. The crescendo of music was growing louder. Liam was obviously showing off his musical abilities.

He wasn't half bad, Holly decided. Since there was no place for her to sit, she inched her way closer to the band. Selecting a small corner of the dance floor, she claimed it, secure in the idea that she was out of the way and could enjoy listening to the band play for a little while.

Without meaning to, as the music seemed to seep deeper and deeper into her, Holly began to sway rhythmically to the beat.

"You know, it's even better if you put down the drink you're holding and move your feet," said a deep male voice behind her.

Surprised, Holly almost dropped the glass. Turning around, she found herself looking at a tall, good-looking male she judged to be somewhere in his late twenties. He had straight blond hair that he wore a little long. The cut succeeded in giving him a rugged, free-range look—and it didn't take an Einstein to realize that he knew it.

His eyes were skimming over her, and Holly felt instantly uncomfortable. "I'll take your word for it," she replied pleasantly and then deliberately turned away from him.

The wrangler didn't—or wouldn't—take the hint and leave. Instead, he poured on a little more of what he had to have assumed was his charm.

"I've always felt that finding things out for yourself is the best way to remember the lesson," he told her. Taking the drink out of her hand, he put it down on the closest flat surface near them.

He'd surprised her. Otherwise, she would have held on harder to her glass. "Maybe I'm not looking to learn any lessons," she countered, reaching around him to pick up her drink.

"Then how about just dancing?" her persistent admirer suggested, removing the drink from her hand for a second time.

"I'm not looking to do that, either," Holly told him firmly, her voice losing its polite edge.

The wrangler moved the drink so that she would have been forced to move into him in order to reach for it again. He blocked her next move, taking a firm hold of her hand.

"That's what your lips say," he told her. "But your hips seem to have other ideas. I'm throwing my vote in with your hips."

Her eyes were icy now, as was her tone. She absolutely hated the idea of causing a scene, but there was no way she was going to allow herself to be plucked up like a piece of candy from a tray, and she could see that this pushy cowboy had more than just dancing on his mind. "You can throw your vote into the Rio Grande, I really don't care."

"C'mon, little lady," he coaxed, grabbing her and pulling her toward him. "Just one dance. You didn't get all dolled up like that just to do an imitation of a wallflower."

"Well, I sure didn't do it to dance with you," she retorted, determined to pull herself free.

"Feisty. I like that," the cowboy declared, laughing as his hold on her tightened, rendering her unable to get away.

For the second time in the space of a few minutes, Holly heard a male voice speak up behind her. "The lady said she's not interested in dancing with you. What part of *no* do you find confusing?"

The way her heart just leaped, even with all the noise, she knew that had to be Ray. How did he get over here so fast? She'd just seen him trying to romance Emma. She sincerely doubted that Emma had said she wasn't interested and had sent Ray away.

"Move on, cowboy," the grabby wrangler ordered between clenched teeth.

With deliberate movements, Ray extricated her

from the wrangler's grasp and placed himself between her and the pushy cowboy.

"You first," Ray countered, keeping his voice even and pleasant. Only the look in his eyes, Holly noted, was steely.

For a second, it looked as if a fight would break out. The wrangler was inches away from trading punches with Ray, but then, at the last moment, he bit off a curse and just waved his hands dismissively at the both of them.

"She ain't worth getting my hair messed up for," the wrangler declared. "Looks as frosty as a frozen cone. She's all yours, cowboy." With that, the offensive wrangler stormed away.

Ray immediately turned his attention to her. There was concern in his eyes when he asked, "That jerk didn't hurt you, did he?"

Touched, Holly shook her head. "No, I'm fine," she assured him, and then she couldn't help asking him, "Where did you come from?"

That grin that always made her heart flip rose to his lips. "Well, initially, according to my mother, I started out as a twinkle in my dad's eye—"

Holly suppressed a laugh and rolled her eyes. "I meant just now. I just saw you halfway across the room with Emma."

The second Ray had looked her way and seen what was going on, he'd felt his temper instantly flaring.

But he kept that part to himself, merely telling her, "You looked like you needed saving." He paused, debating whether or not to say something for her own good. "You know, Doll, you have to be careful about the kind of signals you send out in a place like this," he warned.

"I wasn't sending out signals," Holly protested indignantly. "I was swaying to the music."

"Palm trees sway," Ray corrected. "You were moving your hips in a very inviting way. That creep took you up on the invitation." If he hadn't been here, who knew how far this could have gone before someone would have put a stop to it? He didn't even want to think about what might have happened. He knew that Holly liked to think that she could take care of herself, but the fact was, she wasn't as tough as she liked to think she was. "Next time, be more careful."

Blowing out an exasperated breath, Ray turned on his heel, ready to go back to what he'd been doing before he saw the wrangler coming on to Holly.

"Right, no swaying," Holly promised. And then, grabbing his wrist—and his attention for a second—she flashed him a broad, grateful smile. "Thanks for coming to my rescue."

"Don't mention it." Ray shrugged off her gratitude, just happy he'd been in the right place at the right time. And then, because he was feeling pretty good about the whole thing, he decided not to stomp on her ego. "You probably would have decked him if I hadn't been here, but since I was, I figured I might as well tell that wrangler what he could do with his unsavory advances and his big, grabby hands."

This was nice, she thought. Whether Ray realized it or not—and he probably didn't—he'd just been the white knight to her damsel not-so-in-distress. She allowed herself to pretend that it was for the right reasons: because he cared about her, not as a friend but as a girlfriend.

"How do you know they were unsavory?" she asked.

"Easy. A guy like that only has the unsavory kind," he maintained. And then, looking across the floor, he frowned slightly.

Holly turned around, trying to see what had caught his attention. "What's the matter?"

The frown faded as he shrugged, assuming a disinterested air. "Looks like Emma decided she wanted to dance more than she wanted to wait for me."

And then she saw what he was looking at. Emma was in the arms of Dixon Baker, one of the ranchers. She was looking up at him as if he was the smartest, handsomest man in the room—as well as one of the wealthier ones.

Holly looked at the man beside her. "I'm so sorry I messed up your evening," she apologized, trying very hard not to allow a smile negate what she was saying.

Ray merely shrugged, looking completely unaffected. "No big deal," he told her. "If not Emma, then someone else will come along. I wasn't looking for a lifelong partner, just someone to pass the evening with."

The band was beginning to play another song; this one had a slower tempo than the two numbers that had come just before.

Ray surprised her by turning to face her and saying, "Well, since I seem to temporarily be caught between partners, would you like to dance?"

She would have loved nothing more, but the truth was, dancing was something she had never taken the time to learn—and she didn't want to embarrass herself or him in public like this.

"I don't really dance," she told Ray with a vague, dismissive shrug. She thought that would be the end of it.

But it wasn't.

"I don't think your hips read that memo," Ray told her, his eyes dipping down to look at the area under discussion. "Let's see what they've got," he coaxed, taking her hand in his and drawing her over toward the newly built dance floor.

"I don't think this is a good idea," Holly protested again, although she really liked him taking her hand like that.

But he was going to regret this, she couldn't help thinking. Ray was known to be a good dancer and she couldn't remember the last time she'd moved her feet in anything but a determined, forward pattern, going from one destination to another.

"That's the problem here," he told her with a patient, knowing expression on his face. "You're overthinking this. You're not supposed to think at all," he stressed. "What you're supposed to do is *feel* the rhythm in your bones," he told her, once again bending his head and saying the words into her ear to keep from shouting at her to be heard.

Taking her right hand in his left, gently pressing the small of her back, he brought her up closer to him. Just for a heartbeat, his eyes met hers. "Feel it?" he asked.

What she was feeling wasn't anything she could admit to. It felt like someone had lit a match in her core, and it was spreading out like wildfire to all her extremities at the same time.

Her throat was bone dry as she tried to thrust out a single-word response. There was only one thing she could say in hopes that he couldn't read between the lines. "No."

He spread his hand out, his fingers dipping down below her waist as he tried to get her to mimic his own movements, to mimic the way his hips were moving to the beat of the music.

"Now do you feel it?" he asked, then stressed, "Concentrate."

If possible, her mouth had grown even drier than before. There was no way she could say *anything* until she managed to get some saliva back. So instead, she just nodded because she *did* feel his hips swaying and she did try to mimic the movement.

All this while she was desperately trying to tamp down the flames that threatened to consume her.

Holly raised her head to look at him at the exact moment he looked down. For a second time, their eyes met and held, but this time it seemed to be in a timeless region where clocks had no meaning. Every jump of the pulse was never ending.

What the hell was going on here? The question echoed over and over again in his head. Ray struggled to remind himself that this was Holly, his lifelong friend, the pal he'd played ball with, learned how to rope young colts with, shared secrets and ambitions with. She knew him better than he knew himself— which right now wasn't hard, he thought because at the moment, he felt like a swirling cauldron of confusion. If he didn't know any better, he would have said that he was reacting to Holly, that he was attracted to her—which, of course, wasn't possible.

If anything, it was the dress. It made her look like a different person, not good old Doll but some little hottie he hadn't met yet.

He would have blamed his odd, rather intense reaction on the alcohol he'd consumed. Except he hadn't consumed any alcohol yet. Not even so much as a glass of beer. He'd ordered it, then left it standing on the bar when he saw Emma and decided to set his sights on her.

But, while he'd been making his play—and doing rather well, if he did say so himself—he happened to glance in Holly's direction, completely by accident, and saw the uncomfortable and somewhat distressed expression on her face.

He would have hated himself if he'd ignored his best friend's predicament just to win Emma over for the evening—he doubted if anything that happened between them tonight would have led to something with a longer life expectancy than a bouquet of wildflowers.

The band had just stopped playing when someone accidentally stumbled and bumped into Holly, sending her right into Ray. Their bodies, still close because of the dance, were practically sealed together.

Something hot and formless shot through Ray, jarring him down to his very toes, and he reacted entirely automatically.

There was no other earthly explanation for why his mouth was suddenly pressed against hers.

Chapter Six

This was a dream.

It *had* to be a dream.

But, oh, what a lovely, lovely dream it was, Holly thought as her heart hammered in her chest. She'd had this dream countless times before. Usually she was in bed, and visions of what it would be like to have Ray kiss her would seep into her semiconscious or unconscious state.

Sometimes she even had this dream when she was awake. Then, of course, it would be a daydream, most often on megasteroids. She was capable of creating phenomenally real scenarios for herself.

But all the dreams that had come before this magical moment, be they daydreams or ones she'd had while fast asleep at night, had *never* been this vivid, this incredibly breathtaking. Holly felt as if she'd imbibed not one but several very potent drinks rather than actually leaving her first screwdriver untouched.

She felt that light-headed, that inebriated.

This was divinely delicious, and she intended to savor every single second of it.

Rising up on her toes, flying strictly by instinct, Holly leaned into the kiss, weaving her arms around his neck. Any second now, she was certain that she was going to literally fly away.

Especially when she felt his arms closing around her, sealing her away from the rest of the world. He did such a good job that it seemed as if there was no one else inhabiting this microcosm except the two of them.

Damn, what was going on here? Ray's brain demanded silently.

This *was* Holly, right?

He wasn't sure anymore, but even so, he was fairly certain that it really couldn't be. This woman didn't dress like Holly, didn't act like Holly and most of all, she didn't *taste* the way he'd always assumed that Holly would if he ever thought to fleetingly sample her lips.

The Holly Johnson he knew would have smelled of soap and tasted like some kind of minty toothpaste. Holly was practical. Holly was grounded. By no stretch of the imagination was she some femme fatale who got his pulse running like the lead car in the Indianapolis 500 and his imagination all fired up—as this woman did.

Trying to anchor himself to reality, Ray reluctantly pulled back, separating their lips.

Oh, no, oh, no, don't stop. Please don't stop. I don't want to wake up, not yet, Holly's mind cried.

The next moment, the noise around them shattered the fragile world that had just been created, and reality stormed in.

As subtly as he could, Ray pulled air into his lungs, doing his best not to sound as breathless as he felt. "Thanks for the dance," he murmured.

Holly bobbed her head up and down in response, unable to immediately form any words. Her mouth was far too dry. When she finally could get a few words together and out, she heard herself mumbling the immensely original phrase, "Don't mention it."

Ray regarded her with a mixture of unease and wonder. Aside from her lips having a lethal punch, she sounded a little strange, maybe even disoriented.

There was a lot of that going around, he couldn't help thinking. "You're okay, right?"

"Yeah, sure," she answered hastily, then as her brain stopped revolving at speeds that rivaled the speed of light, she said, "Define 'okay.'"

His eyes never left her face, watching her warily. "I didn't hurt you or anything, did I?"

Oh, you "or anything-ed" me all right, she thought. She was going to remember that exceedingly intimate, wondrous contact for the rest of her life, even if she lived to be two hundred.

"No, you didn't hurt me," she told him with a small, dismissive laugh.

He nodded, taking in her words and trying to find some kind of inner calm for himself. But so far, it just refused to materialize.

What the hell had gotten into him? It wasn't as if he was some oversexed tomcat ready to leap on anything that wandered across his path. He was a decent, fun-loving person who had always treated the women who passed through his life with the utmost respect—and none more so than Holly.

Hell, he doubted he'd ever even been aware of her *being* a woman before tonight. She'd been his friend ever since he'd extended his hand to her the first day she'd come into his classroom, looking like some kind of a lost sheep.

Looking as if she didn't know how to fit in.

He'd felt sorry for her and he hadn't liked the way Margaret Jennings and her girlfriend were making fun of Holly during recess. He'd walked right into the middle of that and offered her his friendship by way of a buffer that day. He'd done it just to be kind—he hadn't counted on really liking her as a pal. But how could he not? They had so much in common. They liked the same things, saw the same movies—and, most important of all, Holly got his jokes.

But never once in all these years had he thought of her as being a girl on her way to womanhood.

Now he couldn't think of anything else.

And he couldn't remember the last time he'd felt even remotely tongue-tied. But right now, words didn't seem to come with any sort of ease.

Instead, they were occurring to him like some randomly shattered mosaic.

"Can I get you anything?" he finally asked, desperate to have something normal to say. "A drink?" he suggested belatedly, latching on to the fact that this was, after all, a saloon.

Holly glanced over toward the table where the grabby wrangler had set her glass down. The screwdriver was still there. She nodded at it now.

"I've already got one, but thanks for the offer."

She took a step toward the table where the drink stood, but Ray shifted so that he was directly in her way.

"I'll get you a fresh one," he told her.

A small smile curved her mouth—the same mouth

that had just been beneath his, he couldn't help thinking, staring at her lips.

"It's not exactly like it spoiled, sitting out on the
table like that. It's not a cut of beef left out in the
hot sun."

Hands on her shoulders, he turned her around to
face the bar, then walked toward it himself. "Yeah,
but that creep touched it, and who knows where else
his hands have been?"

Holly didn't point out that the wrangler had also
touched her when he'd tried to get her to dance with
him. Instead, she followed Ray to the bar and said,
"Thank you, that's very thoughtful."

He laughed, relaxing just a little as they slowly
began to slip back into their customary roles. "Well,
you know me, Doll, I'm a very thoughtful guy."

"Yes," Holly agreed, her eyes skimming over the
back of his head as well as his sturdy, athletic frame.
"You are."

She bit her lip, not wanting to drive him away by
seeming to be too clingy or anything even remotely
like that, but Ray had done what no one else had ever
done for her and he'd done it not just once, but twice,
if she counted their very first meeting.

He'd come to her rescue, and she would always be
grateful to him for that.

"I appreciate your getting that guy to go away," she
told Ray with sincerity. "You didn't have to." After
all, nowhere was it written that he was obligated to
look after her.

"Yeah, I did," Ray contradicted her, waiting for
Brett to work his way back across the bar to their

end of it. "That wrangler didn't look like the type who was going to be satisfied with just one dance."

She laughed, contradicting *him*. "He would have been once he found out how bad a dancer I am."

She wasn't that naive, was she? Turning from the bar, he held up one finger. "Number one, I don't think that a dance was really this guy's end goal, and number two—" he held up a second finger "—you're not as bad a dancer as you keep saying you are. You've got to quit running yourself down all the time like that, Doll."

"I don't run myself down," she said defensively. "I just know my limitations." She shrugged. "I don't believe in bragging and sending up a smoke screen when it comes to what I can or can't do."

There was such a thing as carrying things too far. "All right, say one positive thing about yourself," he challenged her. "Just one, I dare you. Go ahead," he urged.

She wasn't accustomed to listing her own attributes and it took her a minute before she had something she could offer.

"I'm a very nice person," she informed him. She prided herself on that, on being someone who would go out of her way to help others or to make them feel better about themselves.

She liked helping people.

"That's just a given." As far as he was concerned, that was the very definition of Holly. She was exceptionally nice—to everyone. *Even that grabby wrangler,* he thought begrudgingly.

"Not really," she pointed out. "People aren't just

nice by default." It would be a lovely world if that was true, she couldn't help thinking.

"Well, you get that from hanging around with me," he countered with a straight face.

"Oh, really?" She laughed and then, rather than tease him, since she could most definitely still feel the imprint of his lips on hers, Holly relented and said, "Yeah, maybe you're right, I do get that from hanging around with you."

Ray shook his head slightly, his thick black hair moving just enough to make her fingers itch to touch it. "I'm always right," he told her.

"Tell me," she teased. "Do you ever have any trouble getting through doorways with that swelled head of yours?"

"Nope."

Brett came up to him just then. "What'll it be?"

"One screwdriver for the lady—heavy on the juice," he added, remembering how she took the drink.

"Coming right up," Brett promised.

Ray continued facing the bar, keeping his back to Holly. They were going to have to talk about this someday, about what had just happened between them on the dance floor. But "someday" was not now, and he hung on to that, telling himself that exploring what had just happened—why he'd kissed her, why he'd felt lightning zigzagging through his veins when he had and why his stomach still felt as if it had turned into one giant knot—wasn't going to lead to anything good until he knew what to do with any of the answers he might come up with.

"Here," he said, handing her the fresh screwdriver

Brett had just put on the bar. "An uncontaminated vodka and orange juice."

There hadn't *really* been anything wrong with the screwdriver she'd initially ordered. "I hate being wasteful," she confessed, nodding toward the table where she'd left her drink.

"Oh, it's not going to waste," he assured her with a suppressed laughed.

When she turned around to see what he was talking about, he was in time to see Larry Jones, one of the three town drunks, glance around furtively, then swiftly claim the full glass, wrap his tanned fingers around it possessively and make good his escape by moving toward the end of the bar just off the men's room.

"Looks like the sheriff's going to have a boarder at the jailhouse tonight," Ray commented.

"Not on just one drink," Holly protested. She'd never known Rick Santiago to be a stickler about law enforcement to that degree. In general, as a sheriff, he was rather easygoing.

"No," Ray easily agreed. "Not just on one drink." He looked off in the direction that the heavyset man had taken. "But Larry's fast and he's resourceful. The people here are mostly interested in hearing Liam play and deciding how good he is or isn't. They're not going to have a death grip on their glasses of wine or beer or whatever else they're drinking. And despite his weather-beaten look, Larry's pretty fast when he wants to be. And he always wants to be when it comes to something with alcohol in it."

"You've studied him?" she asked in surprise. Why would he do that?

But Ray just shook his head. "I didn't 'study' him, but I do get out more than you do—and I notice things."

She certainly couldn't dispute the last part of his statement, given that she hardly ever went anywhere that wasn't either job related or a necessary extension of her home life—such as to the grocery store for food.

"That you do," she agreed. "That you do. So this is what I've been missing?" she asked, gesturing toward the man they were discussing. Even from here he appeared to have a death grip on the glass he'd lifted. "Watching Larry tie one on?"

Ray laughed softly, the sound winding itself directly under her skin. "That and a few other things," he pointed out.

Such as you, she couldn't help thinking. But out loud, she asked, "Such as?" knowing that he expected her to.

"Such as the way the full moon shimmers along the surface of the lake on some very special nights. And the seductive scent of honeysuckle gliding softly on a June breeze."

The images vividly materialized in her mind's eye. Both, she couldn't help thinking, sounded incredibly romantic.

But she was too much of a realist to believe that her best friend was attempting to verbally seduce *her.* He was just talking, saying the first things that came to his mind.

Still she couldn't help teasing him. "Practicing?" she asked.

"What do you mean, practicing?" he asked, looking at her quizzically.

"You know exactly what I mean," Holly told him. When he made no further comment or response, she decided that a little elaboration was in order. "You're using the lines you were going to say to Emma if you hadn't suddenly come to my rescue."

"I don't have 'lines,'" Ray informed her with a degree of umbrage.

Holly pressed her lips together in an effort to keep her smile back. She only partially succeeded. "My mistake. Although," she couldn't resist adding, "I know a few people who might just disagree with you on that little point."

"Like who?" Ray challenged. It was getting increasingly noisy where they were standing at the bar, so he took hold of her arm and guided her over to a slightly quieter corner.

When they stopped moving, Holly obliged him by doing a rundown of the ten women who comprised his latest circle of wistful admirers and would-be girlfriends.

Finished, she asked, "Have I left anyone out? Anyone current, I mean," she specified. "Otherwise, we could probably just pull up an updated census for the town, listing the single women from, let's say, about eighteen to thirty-five—inclusive. That should cover it, don't you think?"

Ray shook his head in wonder. "You have a hell of an imagination, you know that?"

"And you have a hell of a charming manner about you. It makes it all but impossible for a girl to say no to you." Actually, she sincerely doubted that very many had, although it wasn't something she really wanted to find out for herself. This was definitely a case where ignorance was bliss. "You know, you'll make it hard for yourself to ever really settle down if you keep going through the women around here like they were just disposable tissues."

"I don't go through them like they were disposable tissues," he protested vigorously. "And who says I plan to settle down?"

Granted, she'd never heard him say anything close to that. But men didn't always talk about such things—that would involve talking about emotions, a subject most men avoided like the plague and few knew anything about anyway.

"Most men do," she responded.

"I'm not most men," he pointed out.

No, he wasn't, she thought, and Holly knew it was probably wrong to feel this happy that her best friend had just reiterated his intentions to not form any attachments that lasted for more than a week or three.

But if he planned to drift from woman to woman, that definitely meant he wasn't making plans to marry any one of them, and as long as he wasn't married, he was eligible—she thought. And who knew, anything could happen, right? After all, despite all those dreams, waking or sleeping, she would never have thought that Ray would actually kiss her—and boy, had he *ever*.

Granted, the kiss had begun as an accident, but what really counted was that he didn't instantly pull away. Instead, he'd deepened the almost erotic contact that they'd shared and that, by most definitions, had been an actual, very real kiss that they had enjoyed.

Or, at the very least, that *she* had enjoyed.

Chapter Seven

Holly stifled a yawn as she turned the diner's front doorknob. It was six-thirty the next morning and she hadn't gotten all that much sleep. She'd been far too wired after what had happened to get more than a few small snatches of sleep in between large chunks of just staring at the ceiling—smiling.

She fervently hoped that the diner wouldn't get too busy until her mind had time to kick in. Part of her felt as though she was sleepwalking. With very little encouragement, she could easily curl up on one of the tables and drop off to sleep in an instant.

But that wasn't going to happen. She had a full day ahead of her.

Taking a deep breath, she eased herself into the diner.

Miss Joan was at the far end, wiping down the already clean counter. It was, Holly knew, an idiosyncrasy of hers. She was hoping the woman wouldn't notice her, but she should have known better. Miss Joan seemed to have wraparound vision and could see three hundred and sixty degrees all around her at any given moment.

At the sound of the door opening, the older woman

raised her head and spotted Holly the moment she walked in. With an inward sigh, Holly closed the door behind her.

"So how did it go?" Miss Joan asked.

Holly shrugged out of her jacket, leaving it on the back of a chair for the time being. She got her apron from behind the counter.

"How did what go?" she asked innocently as she tied it around her waist.

The slight frown on Miss Joan's face said she hadn't expected extracting information to be easy.

"Don't get sassy with me, girl. You know what I'm talking about. How did last night go?" Miss Joan asked as she watched Holly intently.

Keeping her mind a blank wasn't working. Miss Joan's question immediately conjured up images of dancing with Ray, of having him hold her in his arms. Most of all, it conjured up that spectacularly magical kiss she'd shared with him.

Just thinking about it now got her pulse moving in double time.

Only extreme focus kept her voice even remotely neutral sounding. "It was okay."

Miss Joan cackled as her eyes narrowed knowingly. "That's not what I heard."

Of course not, Holly couldn't help thinking. This was Miss Joan, the woman who somehow managed to find out everything about everything even before the people who were involved knew about it.

Still, Holly played the innocent a little while longer. "Oh? What have you heard?"

Miss Joan went back to massaging the counter, which was already so clean, it was shining. "That you and that Rodriguez boy were caught up in one hell of a lip-lock on the dance floor right after he got that wrangler to drop his paws off you."

Holly began weaving her way from table to table, filling the sugar dispensers. "Is there *anything* that you don't know?"

Miss Joan never even hesitated in her response. "Well, I don't know why, with that kind of a lead-in, you two didn't just go off and enjoy each other's company for the rest of the evening. Instead, you went home with Laurie and your other friends." The last part sounded almost like an accusation.

Not that Holly had consciously made a choice in the matter, but she was abiding by the rules of proper behavior. "I had agreed to a night out with Laurie and the other girls, so it only stands to reason that I went home with them."

"But you went to Murphy's with Ray," Miss Joan contradicted.

Of course she'd know that, Holly thought. Had it been anyone else except for Miss Joan, she would have been surprised at the extent of the woman's knowledge about her evening. But this *was* Miss Joan, and the woman had eyes everywhere.

"Did you arrange that?" she asked point-blank. When Miss Joan just looked at her, Holly elaborated. "Having Ray pick me up instead of Laurie?"

Miss Joan's expression was inscrutable. "Now, why would I do something like that?"

Holly noticed that the woman didn't deny it, but asked another question, instead, to deflect her attention—or so Miss Joan apparently hoped.

"Oh, I don't know," Holly said loftily. "Maybe for

the same reason you sent over that shimmering blue dress for me to wear."

Miss Joan merely nodded, neither denying nor agreeing with her assumption. Instead, she replied, "You're welcome."

Holly knew in her heart that Miss Joan meant well and that the woman undoubtedly knew that she liked Ray, but she didn't like the idea of someone pulling her strings, even if it *was* Miss Joan. "I don't recall saying thank-you."

Miss Joan looked up from the counter, her expression just as unreadable now as it was a moment ago. "But you will, girl," she predicted. "If you've got a brain in your head, you will."

She was being too sensitive, Holly thought. There was no point in pretending around Miss Joan. The woman had a way of being able to see through lies, even small ones.

"The dress really *was* beautiful," Holly finally had to admit.

"No, *you* were beautiful," Miss Joan corrected. "The dress was just sparkly material. *You* brought it into the spotlight, gave it life," the woman insisted. "That Rodriguez boy is just like a horse. You've got to lead him to the watering hole and stick his face in the water before he catches on and does what he's supposed to do."

She was afraid to ask what Miss Joan thought he was supposed to do. The older woman was just outspoken enough to tell her, and Holly really wasn't sure that she was up to hearing Miss Joan lay out her future for her—a future that hadn't a chance in hell of actually happening.

So instead, Holly asked her, "What's the lunch special for today so I'll know what to put down when I do the menu board?"

"Anything that Angel wants it to be," Miss Joan said matter-of-factly.

The cook had carte blanche as far as Miss Joan was concerned. Angel had been with her a little more than a year now, and Gabe's wife was a veritable miracle worker when it came to creative cooking and working with the ingredients that were available.

"She'll let you know what she's making when she gets here," Miss Joan assured her. "But you're going to have to set up the menu board a lot earlier today because you won't be here for lunch."

Holly looked up sharply. Now what? "Why won't I be here?"

"Because I'm recruiting you," Miss Joan said simply. Then she glanced at her to see if Holly understood. "Don't you remember what today is?"

Holly thought for a moment. "It's December first," she said, watching Miss Joan's face to see if there was something more, something she'd apparently neglected to remember.

Miss Joan sighed and rolled her eyes. "You did forget," she concluded, then proceeded to jar her memory. "It's also the first Saturday of the month. I can remember when you were a little girl and you used to count the days until the first Saturday in December," she said with a touch of sadness.

Holly racked her brain for a moment, trying to connect the dots—and then it dawned on her. "Are you talking about getting the town's Christmas tree?"

"Well, what do you know?" Miss Joan laughed,

looking at her pointedly. "You remembered. Maybe there's hope for you yet, girl."

This was the first time that the woman had invited her to come along on the tree-hunting expedition. Holly still wasn't completely sure that she had guessed correctly. "You want me to go with you?"

Miss Joan made a vague half shrug, raising one very thin shoulder and then letting it drop carelessly.

"I thought that maybe it was time for you to make the trek, put that young back into it," she told Holly crisply. "I told the rest of this year's crew to be here by eleven so that we could all set out together. I figure that it's going to be tricky," she added.

Holly knew that each year, Miss Joan would ask a few men she thought to be best qualified for the job to come along. The useful ones she asked year after year. The ones who hadn't measured up to her standards, she left behind the following year.

Just what did she mean by tricky? Holly wondered. "Why?"

Miss Joan looked at her incredulously. "Do you ever *look* out this window, girl?" the other woman asked. As if to illustrate her point, Miss Joan walked to the front of the diner and gestured toward the view that was outside and in the distance. "See anything that gets your attention?" she asked in a tone that was devoid of any emotion other than put-upon patience.

Holly crossed over to where the older woman was standing and glanced out the window as she was told. She didn't see anything out of the ordinary. It was the same barren expanse of land it always was.

"Take in the *big* picture," Miss Joan urged when Holly made no response.

"That's where you're going to get the tree, right?" Holly asked, referring to the mountain in the distance.

"That's where *we're* going, yes," Miss Joan confirmed. Her tone indicated that she was impatiently waiting for the proverbial lightbulb to go off in Holly's head.

"I—" Holly was about to say she didn't know what she was looking for and then she realized what Miss Joan was referring to. "There's snow on the mountain."

"Finally. I was beginning to think we needed to have you fitted for glasses."

It didn't snow very often in this part of Texas, certainly never *in* Forever. But the mountains were up high enough to have received a dusting of it if there was any to fall, which there obviously was.

"Mick's going to have to put chains on the truck tires—if he's got any chains to put on," Miss Joan qualified. "That man doesn't believe in being prepared for any contingencies. He just figures if he needs something, he can get it when the time comes." Miss Joan shook her head. "If he doesn't have any chains, we're going to have to drive up really carefully."

Now that she thought about it, Holly started getting excited about the event. "You really want me to come with you?"

"Thought maybe you'd like a turn. You're pretty levelheaded—most of the time," Miss Joan qualified. "And the town's going to need someone to pick out the tree if I'm not around."

Holly looked at the woman sharply. "Why wouldn't you be around?" she asked, suddenly growing concerned. "Miss Joan, are you feeling all right? There's nothing wrong, is there? Something you're not telling me?" she added, prodding the woman.

"There's lots of things I'm not telling you, girl," Miss Joan said. "But on the subject of my health, there's nothing wrong."

Then what was with the drama? Holly didn't understand. "Then why—"

"Because I'm not going to live forever," Miss Joan said practically. "Nobody does, and after I'm gone, I want to be sure that this town always has the best damn tree that can be found on the mountain every year."

"You're not going anywhere," Ray told the owner of the diner, walking in on Miss Joan's last sentence. "You know that you're just too ornery to die," he reminded the older woman.

Miss Joan turned to look at him. "Well, it's not going to be anytime soon, at any rate." She wiped her hands. "You want the usual?" she asked Ray. When he nodded, rather than getting it herself, she turned to Holly. "Get Ray the usual—it's on the house this morning, seeing as how I'm going to be making use of that strong back of yours," the woman informed him.

Out of the corner of her eye, she noticed that Holly had made no effort to move and fetch Ray either the coffee or his customary jelly doughnut.

"Somebody glue your feet to the floor, girl?" Miss Joan asked.

Holly was only vaguely aware that Miss Joan had said anything at all to her. Her mind had stopped processing words right after she heard that he was going on the expedition with them.

"You're coming with us to get the tree?" she asked Ray, needing to make sure that she'd heard correctly.

"No, I've decided to take a lover and I'm seducing him with my jelly doughnuts," Miss Joan deadpanned. "Yes, he's coming with us. That's why his breakfast—which is a damn unhealthy one if you ask me, but then, you didn't ask me—is on the house," the woman concluded, then shifted her attention to Holly. "Now, are you going to get his coffee and doughnut or have you taught the doughnuts to come when you call?"

That made her finally come to. Holly turned on her heel and moved quickly across the floor, rounding the counter so she could get to the giant coffee urn and fill up a cup for Ray.

Miss Joan was doing her best to sound gruff, Holly thought, but it didn't matter what she said or how she said it, that quirky woman had just created what had to be the perfect day for her. They were going on the mountain to bring back a giant Christmas tree for the town, and not only was she going to be part of the group that selected the tree—or, more accurately, part of the group that rubber stamped Miss Joan's selection—she was going to be doing it with Ray.

"You grin any wider, girl, it's going to slow down your progress considerably," Miss Joan warned her.

"Yes, ma'am, no grinning," Holly automatically agreed. Right now, she would have been hard-pressed to think of a single thing that Miss Joan could ask her to do that she'd turn down.

"Now, did I say that?" Miss Joan asked. "I said, and I'm quoting now, 'any wider.' That means keep it to a safe level where you're not catching bugs and working with a windchill factor." Three more men came in and Miss Joan frowned as she looked at her watch. "Can't none of you boys tell time? I said eleven, not seven. I know they rhyme, but they're four hours apart."

Eli, one of Ray's older brothers, slid onto a stool at the counter. He nodded a greeting at the older woman, carefully removing his hat in her presence.

Miss Joan smiled at him. She had always had a soft spot in her heart for Eli. She considered him to be the most sensitive of the Rodriguez brothers.

"Maybe we're just all too excited to wait," Eli told her. "It's kind of like when we were little and waiting for Santa Claus to come. It felt like time just stretched out endlessly before us."

Miss Joan looked down the bridge of her nose at the strapping young man. "If you still believe in Santa Claus, Eli, I think we might just have ourselves a problem here."

"Don't spoil their fun, Joannie. If they want to believe in Santa Claus, let 'em," Harry, Miss Joan's husband, said as he came around to her other side and put his arms around her, then pressed a kiss to her cheek. He'd walked into the diner not more than three minutes ago, slipping in quietly as was his custom. He liked to say that he enjoyed watching his wife in action.

Miss Joan didn't look overly happy as she pulled free of his embrace after a rather long moment. "What did I tell you about calling me Joannie in public?" she asked in almost a snarled whisper.

"You said not to," Harry dutifully recited. "But honey, these boys and Holly—" he nodded in her direction "—are like family. No need to be embarrassed around family," her husband teased.

"A lot you know," Miss Joan quipped. If Laurie had been here instead of late the way she customarily was—she'd assigned the girl to start her shift half an hour earlier than she was actually supposed to, thereby breaking even—her nickname would have found itself posted everywhere. "What are you doing here, anyway?"

"Thought I'd come along," Harry told her. "Help you make up your mind about which tree to bring back. You know, do the kind of things a husband is supposed to do for his wife."

"Said the man who stares at three pairs of black socks in the morning, trying to decide which pair to put on. You're staying here, Harry," she informed him in her no-nonsense voice. "You'll just hold me up and I don't want to have to be worrying about you up there."

"No reason to worry," Harry told her. "I'm as sure-footed as a goat."

Miss Joan almost hooted. "An old goat," she specified. "And I want to be sure that you just keep on getting older—and you won't if you fall and break that fool neck of yours. End of discussion. You're staying here."

"Then you are, too," Harry informed his wife mildly. "I can be just as stubborn as you, Joannie."

Rick had joined them at the counter, looking for nothing more than a fortifying black cup of coffee. Holly automatically poured him a cup and set it down in front of him.

"No offense, Harry, but not even God is as stubborn as Miss Joan is," Rick told the woman's husband. "There's no shame in retreating if it's from Miss Joan," he guaranteed. "We've all done it."

"Yeah, but you're not married to her," Harry pointed out.

"And you are, which already proves the kind of steadfast man you are. Now, you can stand here, arguing with her and have her argue back, but we'll be losing precious time because she's not budging and if you don't budge, there's not going to be a tree in the town square until Easter," Holly predicted, throwing in her two cents and hoping to make a difference. "Do it for the town, Harry," she urged. "We need you to back off."

"Don't you be telling my man what to do," Miss Joan declared, her hands fisted at her waist and creating a formidable image despite her thin frame. "You can come, Harry. Just stay in the truck. There's snow on that mountain and I don't want you falling and breaking something I've taken a shine to," she told her husband with a surprisingly sexy smile.

"Whatever you say, darlin'," Harry readily agreed. It was obvious that when she looked at him like that, he lost all desire to argue even for a second.

"Okay, that's settled," Miss Joan declared, relieved. She turned toward Ray and a couple of the other men who had shown up, bleary-eyed and mumbling. "One of you boys go get Mick out of bed and tell him we need chains for our tires. And if he doesn't have them, he damn well better find a way to make them—quick," she warned.

"I'll handle it," Cash volunteered.

"Good." Miss Joan nodded at her stepson and half

a second later, was on to the next detail of her very detailed list. The others all listened. Everyone knew better than to interrupt Miss Joan once she got rolling.

Chapter Eight

Miraculously, Mick Henley, Forever's resident—and only—mechanic, did have not only one but several sets of tire chains. They were packed away in his storeroom where they'd been ever since they'd made the move with him years ago from his previous shop in Utah. Consequently, there were enough sets of tire chains for Miss Joan's 4x4 and Joe Lone Wolf's truck as well as the flatbed truck that Miss Joan had specially requisitioned and brought in from a Pine Ridge garage the day before.

But getting the trucks' tires outfitted took time. So while Holly waited for the vehicles to be prepared, Miss Joan asked her to continue waiting on the customers who came in to the diner to grab a quick breakfast or to treat themselves to a slow, leisurely one because today was Saturday and they had no place to be.

Holly tried to bank down the excited feeling that insisted on pulsating through her, but she wasn't having all that much luck.

Added to that, it seemed unusually crowded to her for an early Saturday morning, and Laurie was already twenty minutes late.

Holly knew everyone by name as well as by their orders. Most people, she'd discovered shortly after taking this job, were predictable. If they found something they liked, they stayed with it rather than experimenting and sampling other things.

She supposed, as she juggled two orders, that she was the same way herself. In her case, it wasn't food that won her steadfast allegiance, it was love.

Specifically, it was love of Ray.

Looking back over her short life, Holly couldn't remember even having so much as a passing crush on any other boy or man from the very first time she'd laid eyes on the youngest of the Rodriguez clan.

And she sincerely doubted that she ever would.

Every so often, Holly glanced out the side window to see how Mick was doing as he worked at getting the tires fitted with the proper chains. Her mind vacillated between the customers she was serving inside the diner and what was going on just *outside* the diner. She was so preoccupied that she came close to refilling the space next to Gabe Rodriguez's cup rather than aiming the spout of her coffeepot *into* his empty coffee cup.

She flushed when she realized that Ray's brother was moving her hand an inch to the left so that his cup could catch the black liquid that was about to come pouring out.

"Oh, God, I'm so sorry, Gabe," Holly cried, dismayed at what she'd almost done. By not paying attention, she could have easily burned his hand. Damn it, she was usually better at juggling tasks than this, she silently upbraided herself.

"No harm done," Gabe told her cheerfully. "What's

got your attention so riveted?" he asked, glancing out the same window she'd just been looking through.

"I'm just waiting for Mick to finish putting chains on Miss Joan's 4x4 and the other vehicles," she told one of Forever's three resident deputies.

Holly had piqued his interest. "Why does Miss Joan need chains? Is she planning on taking a trip?" Gabe asked, this time turning his stool around to face the same direction Holly had been looking. "Oh, wait," he suddenly recalled before he could see exactly what the mechanic was doing. "Today's the day she picks out the town's tree, isn't it?" Gabe's eyes shifted back to the flustered waitress who was hovering over him and he made a calculated guess. "And you're one of the people she picked to go with her this year, aren't you?" When Holly bobbed her head up and down, Gabe asked, "Who else is going this year, do you know?"

She rattled off a few names, then added, "and Ray," doing her best to sound nonchalant, or at least indifferent—and fairly certain that her future did *not* lie in the field of acting.

But if Gabe suspected that she had a crush on his brother, or any feelings for Ray at all for that matter, he gave no indication.

Instead, the deputy continued to make polite conversation. "Dad said Ray seemed to be in an all-fired hurry to be somewhere this morning when he left the house." Specifically, the senior Rodriguez had called him to ask if he knew what was up with Ray and why he'd actually gotten up and gotten dressed so early in the morning without being nagged into it. Of all of them, Ray was the one who liked to sleep in the most.

"So it takes a Christmas-tree expedition to get Sleeping Beauty out of his bed," Gabe marveled. "I would have said that it would have taken nothing less than a shotgun aimed at his toes to get Ray moving before dawn." But even as he said it, Gabe had serious doubts that getting Ray up early actually had anything to do with selecting the right Christmas tree.

From what he'd heard from a couple of his friends who'd been at Murphy's last night, Gabe was far more inclined to believe that his younger brother had actually been motivated by the promise that his best friend was going on the expedition, as well.

The slight noise made by the bell that Miss Joan had hanging at the front door instantly caught Holly's attention. The first thought she had was that someone had been sent in to fetch her.

But it was only Laurie coming on duty.

Good, that meant she could go outside and wait for Mick to finish there.

Her joy was short-lived. The other waitress looked bleary-eyed and seemed as if she was having trouble focusing. Instead of going behind the counter for her apron, Laurie sank down on the closest empty stool and propped her elbows up on the counter. She used her hands in turn to prop up her head.

"Coffee," she called out to Holly. "Please," she added plaintively. "Pour it straight into my veins if possible." As she leaned her head harder against her upturned palm, she made a miscalculation. The next thing she knew, her chin slipped and it all but made contact with the counter, jolting her into a state of almost wakefulness as her eyes flew open.

Holly was quick to bring her the requested coffee, black as midnight.

"Hey, careful before you knock yourself out," Holly warned, witnessing the near collision of chin and counter. She slid the cup and saucer directly in front of the other waitress.

Laurie eyed her accusingly. "Why do you look so wide awake?" she asked. Before Holly could say anything, Laurie thought of an answer. "Don't tell me you actually went into your house when we dropped you off there last night."

Holly shrugged, not quite following what the other waitress was getting at. "Okay, I won't," she agreed, then couldn't help asking, "Why won't I?"

"Because none of us did, that's why." She thought of her own evening. "Jimmy Evans swung by to pick me up in his Jeep after I dropped off the other girls." Laurie managed a wide, wistful smile.

"What time *did* you get in?" Holly asked.

Laurie looked at her watch, trying to focus on the numbers and finding that her eyes weren't up to the task just yet. "What time is it now?" she asked Holly.

"You didn't go home at all, did you?" Holly guessed. "You just stopped off to change before coming here, right?"

"Nobody likes a smart-aleck," Laurie mumbled. The next moment, she seemed even worse than when she'd first walked in. "Take my shift, Holly," she begged suddenly.

"I can't," Holly said, thinking of the afternoon that lay ahead. She really didn't want to miss being part of that, especially since Ray was going to be part of it, as well.

But Laurie wasn't ready to give up. "Please? Pretty please?" she begged more urgently. "I'll give you my firstborn."

"Tempting though that is, I really can't. Miss Joan wants me to go with her." And that was the main reason she wasn't going to stay and take Laurie's shift as well as her own. Because when Miss Joan told you to come, you did exactly that, even if there were obstacles in your way.

"Miss Joan wants a waitress who's conscious," Laurie pointed out. Holding her cup with both hands, she all but drained it, then waited for the caffeine to kick in. It didn't. Impatience coupled itself with nervousness. "You *have* to take my shift, Holly. If I don't get some sleep and soon, I'm going to die," she lamented.

"Correction. If you try to palm off your shift onto someone else, you're going to die," Miss Joan said, walking into the diner. As was her habit, she'd zeroed in on the conversation that concerned her most. Her hazel eyes shifted toward Holly. "We're ready. Come outside," she instructed.

She really, really wanted to go, but there was someone in distress right in front of her. How could she have a good time, knowingly abandoning Laurie in this miserable state?

"But Laurie doesn't feel well," Holly pointed out, unhappily resigning herself to take the other waitress's place as well as waiting on customers in her station. "She needs to go home."

"Laurie is hungover," Miss Joan corrected. "What she needs is to man up so she can do her shift as well as yours." Miss Joan paused to take the other waitress's chin in her hand, closely examined the young woman's face from both sides, then released it. "You'll live," she told Laurie crisply. "Nobody ever dies from a hangover—they just want to," she added with a knowing look. "Now get out there," she said, addressing the command to Holly. "We roll in less than five."

Holly knew that Miss Joan was as good as her word, and if she wasn't out there on time as ordered, the small convoy would head out without her. She didn't want them to.

Quickly making up her mind, Holly removed her apron and grabbed the jacket she'd left slung over the back of an unoccupied chair. Saturdays were casual, and Miss Joan allowed her waitresses to wear jeans, which was lucky for her, Holly thought, hurrying into her jacket and trying to keep up with the older woman as she walked out of the diner.

"Were you ever in the military, Miss Joan?" Holly asked, quickening her pace. In the background, she could hear Miss Joan's husband laughing at her question.

"I tried to enlist once, when I was a lot younger," she admitted, then deadpanned wryly, "But they told me I was too tough for them."

Holly could readily believe it.

"Good luck!" she heard Gabe call out after her. She turned and waved at him just before she crossed the threshold.

Holly couldn't help wondering if the deputy actually thought she was going to need luck or if he'd just said that automatically.

The next moment, Gabe and the possibly cryptic meaning behind his words were stored away and forgotten.

She saw Ray standing outside the cab of the flat-bed truck, holding the driver's-side door open.

"You're riding with Ray," Miss Joan told her in the no-nonsense voice she used when she wasn't about to tolerate the slightest argument or contradiction from anyone about anything. "I told him to drive the flat-bed truck. The rest of you have your assigned positions," she declared, looking over the seven other men she had tapped for the job of securing the town's annual Christmas tree this year. "Okay, gentlemen—and Holly—let's roll," she ordered, getting into her own vehicle and waiting for her stepson to climb into the passenger seat beside her.

As she'd predicted, the small convoy of vehicles was heading toward the mountain in the distance in less than five minutes.

Not one of them would have dreamed of keeping Miss Joan waiting.

"Miss Joan is running this like a military operation," Ray commented as they were approaching their destination.

"Miss Joan has a tendency to run everything like a military operation," Holly reminded him.

Ray nodded. "Maybe she was a military brat," he guessed. It was a possibility.

No one in town knew very much about the woman's background before she came to Forever, and Miss Joan wasn't very forthcoming unless she specifically wanted to be—which most of the time, she didn't.

"I think it's more likely that she just likes the precision that the military stands for, so she emulates it. That and she likes ordering people around," Holly added with a grin. "But she's got a good heart, so I guess it all balances out in the end."

It was a known fact that if anyone was in trouble, or found themselves with their back against a wall, Miss Joan would quietly come to their aid, asking for nothing in return.

Holly watched as they came closer to the end of their journey. Her sense of excitement growing, she suddenly turned to Ray and asked, "What's snow like?"

The question caught him entirely off guard. He was sure he hadn't heard Holly correctly. "What?"

She decided to rephrase her question. Maybe Ray hadn't experienced snow, either. He certainly had never mentioned anything about snow to her. "Do you know what snow's like?"

He looked at her as if one of the screws holding her brain in place had come loose. "Of course I do." And then the implied part of her question suddenly hit him. "You don't?"

Holly shrugged. She'd made a mistake asking. But this was Ray and they shared all kinds of thoughts with each other. She knew he hadn't meant to make her feel dumb for asking about snow. She really hoped that he didn't think she was odd because she'd never held snow in her hand.

"No," she answered quietly.

Ray thought she was pulling his leg. He was sufficiently far enough behind Miss Joan's truck not to worry about hitting the vehicle. He looked at his best friend for a second before turning back to diligently watching the road.

He wanted to get this straight.

"You've never touched snow?" he asked her incredulously.

"Never mind," Holly said, waving away her initial question. "Forget I ever said anything." She shouldn't have spoken up. Sometimes she was just too honest, too trusting.

"No," he insisted. "You started this and now you've got me curious. I can't believe you don't know what snow feels like. It's snowed on the mountain before," he pointed out. "I can remember at least a couple of other times when there was a snowfall."

"Maybe." She wasn't about to dispute that part of it, but it had never snowed down here, at Forever's altitude. "But I've never gone up to the mountain before."

He couldn't believe it. How oblivious had he been to have missed this piece of information? He tried to recall if they'd ever talked about anything having to do with snow before and realized that the subject had never come up.

"Why not?" he asked.

She looked at him and realized that he was serious about getting an answer to his question. "Well, from the time I was eight, I was always busy helping my mother. That's when my father—"

"Died," Ray filled in, chagrined. He'd certainly walked into that one with both feet, he thought, annoyed with his lack of tact—and memory. "Yeah, I remember now. I'm sorry."

She never allowed him to beat himself up. "Nothing to be sorry about," she told Ray. "After all, I wasn't the only kid who lost a parent. You lost your mother," she said quietly, just to prove her point.

"Yeah, and you were there for me for that," he recalled.

Looking back, he knew he wouldn't have been able to make it if it hadn't been for Holly. She'd been the one friend he'd unloaded all his feelings, all his anger on. She was the one friend who had seen him cry while he'd kept a stiff upper lip around everyone else, including his own family. Holly knew him better than anyone else.

"You know," Ray admitted contritely. "You've always been a much better friend to me than I've ever been to you."

"It's not a contest, Ray. But if you want to be there for me now…" she said as he brought the flatbed to a halt. Miss Joan had already stopped her own vehicle. The plan was to go on foot from here.

"Yeah?" he asked, waiting for Holly to finish.

She was nervous about walking in snow for the first time. She didn't want to make a fool of herself. "If I start to slip, hold me up so I don't embarrass myself in front of the others."

He grinned at her just before he jumped out of the cab. "I've got your back, Doll," he promised.

Heartened, Holly pushed open the door on her side of the truck and looked down at the pristine blanket of white below her. It looked harmless enough. How bad could it be?

Okay, she thought, here went nothing.

She jumped out. The next second, she felt her boots sinking into the snow, searching for bottom.

The gasp escaped her lips inadvertently.

Chapter Nine

"Ray!"

Every fiber, nerve ending and bone in Ray's body went on high alert, galvanizing and becoming hard.

Standing on the other side of the flatbed truck's cab, unable to see Holly, all he had to go on was her voice, and it was half panicky, half bewildered.

Before his imagination had time to go into high gear, envisioning everything from a sinkhole to a lumbering bear or ravenous coyote, Ray had rounded the front of the truck and hurried over to her side.

It wasn't hard to see what the problem was. Holly couldn't sustain a foothold.

Grabbing her hand, he kept Holly from sinking into the snow as well as from falling, face-first, into a snowdrift. Aside from keeping her upright, Ray was also doing his level best not to laugh at the surprised, distressed expression on her face.

Holly hadn't been kidding, he realized. This really was her first experience with snow.

"Takes some getting used to," he told her.

"No kidding," she muttered under her breath, annoyed with herself.

"You two coming, or would you rather keep trying

to make snow angels?" Miss Joan called over to them as the rest of the crew gathered around her, waiting for instructions. Every group needed a leader who organized things, and Miss Joan was clearly theirs.

"We're coming," Holly responded, raising her voice. Taking small steps, she held her arms out for balance, trying to get her "snow legs" so that she could move forward without looking like a flailing baby sparrow trying to fly.

"You're getting there," Ray said, encouraging her. He took hold of one of her hands to give her an anchor in hopes of keeping her upright.

"If you say so," Holly answered, not bothering to suppress her own grin.

She supposed that there were some major advantages to the snow after all. Anything that got Ray to make some sort of physical contact with her was definitely not all bad.

"Stick together," Miss Joan instructed. The warning was intended for the group, but she was looking specifically at Holly when she issued the order. "I don't want to have to be the one to ask the sheriff to bring in a search party out here. As long as you make sure you keep a couple of people in sight at all times, you're not going to get lost," she said, then ordered, "Okay, buddy up and let's get busy. Anyone find a tree worth considering, holler for the others. Remember, we need to find this year's tree pretty fast. The last thing we want is to be out here when it gets dark."

With Miss Joan's words ringing in their ears, the men and Holly all fanned out, each pair moving in a slightly different direction than the others.

"They all look so pretty," Holly noted, looking

around at all the majestic specimens that reached out toward the sky before them. "How do we choose just one?" she asked Ray. To her, the very first one they looked at seemed perfect.

"Well, in this particular case, size does matter," Ray told her, dismissing the tree she was looking at. He estimated that at its highest point, it was barely ten feet tall.

"Okay, then how about that one?" Holly asked, selecting another, far taller tree.

"Better," he agreed expansively as he approached the one she'd picked.

"And it's certainly tall enough," Holly needlessly pointed out.

"Right," he agreed; however, she'd overlooked something again. "But don't forget," he reminded her. "We've also got to be able to transport the tree back to town."

One glance at the gargantuan tree was enough to make him realize that there was no way it was going to be brought back to town by utilizing the flatbed truck, even if the surface of that flatbed *was* extralong.

"Unless, of course, we find a way to roll it down the mountain," Ray deadpanned.

"Point taken," she replied. They began walking again, searching for a new candidate. "I guess finding the right tree is going to be a lot like the story of the three bears."

Ray stared at her, not having the faintest clue what she was talking about. "Come again?"

"You know," she prompted. "Not too big, not too small, it has to be *just right*," Holly said in the high-pitched, singsong voice she used whenever she read storybooks to her niece.

"Glad you're getting the hang of this," Miss Joan congratulated them sarcastically as she joined them momentarily to see how they were doing. "Now see if you can find something that qualifies."

"Yes'm," Ray answered for both of them.

He was sorely tempted to salute the older woman but he had a feeling that he'd regret the veiled foray into sarcasm. When it came to utilizing sarcasm, Miss Joan knew no match.

FINDING JUST THE right tree turned out to be harder than she would have thought, Holly discovered. It was difficult finding a tree amid all the tall ones that was small enough to be transported, yet large enough for the town square. Predominantly, large enough for everyone who wanted to decorate at least a little of the tree. The one thing that Miss Joan insisted on was that the tree be large enough for everyone in Forever to feel as if it was actually theirs.

Finally, after trudging around for the better part of almost two hours, they found a worthy candidate. Joe Lone Wolf, the sheriff's deputy, was the one who found it in the end, and he called over the others in the group to get their vote.

"No doubt about it, it's a beautiful specimen," Holly told him appreciatively, shading her eyes as she looked up the length of the tree. "It's tall and full," she noted, glancing toward Miss Joan to see what she thought of it. "Just like you specified."

Never one to become effusive even when faced with absolute perfection, Miss Joan nodded casually.

"I guess it'll have to do. Okay, boys," she declared, turning toward several of the men she'd recruited who had come up on previous expeditions, "you know what to do. Now get busy and do it!"

"What can I do?" Holly asked, stepping forward.

"Once they chop that baby down, I'll need all of you to load the tree onto the flatbed. As for right now," Miss Joan continued, looking at the waitress, "you can get out of the way—unless you want to risk getting hit by a stray branch."

Ray pulled her back as Cash and a couple of the others returned with the battery-powered saws they'd brought up with them.

"Just watch," he told Holly.

Holly frowned. She'd never liked standing on the sidelines while others did the work, and she wasn't very good at it.

"I feel like a bump on a log," she complained bitterly to Ray.

"Well, you don't look like one," he said with a laugh, tossing her a crumb. "And besides, if you don't do what Miss Joan tells you to, you know she's going to chew you out."

Holly signed. She knew he was right.

The area around the tree that had been picked out came alive with activity as the men set up their workspace. Holly did as she was told and moved back, out of the way. Since more and more seemed to be going on with chips of wood flying every which way, Holly continued to move farther and farther back.

When she suddenly missed her footing, a small cry escaped her lips and she started to fall backward. Hearing her, Ray came to her rescue.

Or tried to.

This time, though, rather than him stopping her, she caused him to lose his balance and when she did fall backward, she took him with her.

Despite tensing his body, Ray wound up falling on top of her.

The wind was knocked out of both of them. So much so that for a split second, all either one of them could do was lay there, two bodies pressed up against each other, their faces less than an inch apart.

But rather than grow colder, lying on the snow the way they were—especially Holly—they grew warmer.

Decidedly warmer.

So much so that Holly was fairly certain that she was sinking deep into the snow, the newly created hole forming thanks to the rise in her body temperature.

"Are you all right?" Ray asked her, still somewhat stunned—and still making no effort to get up.

Holly stared up into his eyes. "Never better," she heard herself whisper. She was surprised that her words were even marginally audible, competing the way they were with the sound of her heart slamming wildly against her ribcage.

"I didn't hurt you, did I?" he asked, concerned.

Her eyes on his, Holly slowly moved her head from side to side. All of her felt as if it was on fire.

Was this what it was like, she couldn't help wondering. What it was like to want someone, *really* want someone?

She had never been intimate with anyone; there never seemed to be a point. She had never cared about anyone enough to get to that incredibly special, incredibly private place inhabited by only two people at a time. Her heart had been lost to Ray at a very young age and she had never even made an effort to reclaim it.

Now she knew why.

Because she would have missed out on this, on the way adrenaline was rushing through her body because they were so wondrously close to one another.

And it felt sinfully intimate.

Ray knew he should get up now, before anyone looked over in their direction and saw this. Before Miss Joan strode over and made one of her wry, cryptic remarks, asking how this helped the process of securing the town's Christmas tree.

Right now, this was still an accident, a result of improper shifting of bodies. If it continued, well, then it was something more, not the least of which would be his taking advantage of the situation.

But the rest of his body was not responding to what his mind was telling it to do. Rather than jumping to his feet, he continued lying over Holly, not to protect her but to savor and absorb the heat of her body seeping into his despite the layers of clothing that were between them. It was almost as if the intense body heat he was feeling was melting away everything that lay in its path.

The next moment, rather than get up, rather than offering her his hand, Ray caught himself framing her face and bringing his mouth down on hers.

If it was possible to experience a Fourth of July moment in the beginning of December, then that was what this felt like.

The taste of her sweet mouth had rockets exploding in the air all around him. The fireworks only made him deepen the kiss, only made him want her more.

Want her?

What was *wrong* with him?

This was Holly he was reacting to, Holly he found himself wanting with every fiber of his being. Holly, who had been like another sister to him, Holly, who he had gone skinny-dipping with a hundred years ago when they were both kids.

And yet, this wasn't Holly at all, at least not *that* Holly. This was someone who stirred him on a level that not a single other woman ever had yet.

And it scared him.

Scared him, but not enough to flee, not even enough to immediately pull his mouth away.

At least, not until he heard Miss Joan say, "You find a new way to apply CPR, boy? Or did the two of you forget the right way to make snow angels? If that's the problem, you're supposed to be next to each other, not on top of each other," she reminded Miguel's youngest son.

Ray immediately jumped to his feet, extending his hand to Holly.

Embarrassed, fighting to keep the color of her complexion down to a subdued pink rather than a blazing red, Holly took the offered hand, wrapped her fingers around it and quickly gained her feet.

"I slipped," she told Miss Joan, deliberately avoiding the older woman's eyes.

The latter nodded knowingly. "I can see that," she commented, her voice pregnant with meaning.

"Think the two of you can stay upright long enough to help carry this tree onto the flatbed?" she asked, looking from one to the other.

"Of course I can," Holly said with more conviction than she felt.

Inside, she felt as if she was entirely made of whipped cream.

"Just lead the way," Ray told the older woman, his voice sounding very stiff and formal. He didn't like being embarrassed and Miss Joan had succeeded in doing just that.

"Oh, I can lead all right," Miss Joan assured them. "But can you follow?" she asked, her hazel eyes sweeping over them meaningfully.

"Sure," Holly said quickly.

"No problem," Ray bit off.

Miss Joan laughed under her breath—none too quietly—as if to say, "We'll see about that," but for once she kept the words to herself.

Cash had backed up the flatbed so that it was as parallel to the felled tree as possible. There was enough space all around the specimen for the men and Holly to adequately surround the tree.

Miss Joan ordered everyone to squat down and get one arm and shoulder under their section of the Scotch pine. "All right, everyone, put your backs into it!" she instructed.

The first effort was less than successful, accompanied by a cacophony of grunts and groans. "You call that trying?" she demanded, clearly disappointed with their combined effort. "A bunch of kindergarteners could do better than that."

"Maybe we should wait until you bring them in," one of the men, Gary Walker, grumbled.

"This isn't a dialogue, Walker," Miss Joan snapped. "Unless you want to be the one to tell the kids in Forever why they don't have a tree this year. No? I didn't think so. Okay, now let's see you give it a *real* try this time," she ordered, her sharp gaze taking everyone in. "Get in under the branches, wrap your hand around the section of truck next to you and let's see you do it. On the count of three this time," she said, then proceeded to do a countdown. "One. Two. *Three!*"

This time, the trunk cleared the ground. The tree wavered and looked as if it was going to go back down again, but somehow, between them all, they managed to stabilize it and with a chorus of louder grunts and groans, they finally got the tree loaded onto the flatbed.

Exhausted, the ten people Miss Joan had selected to be part of her crew leaned against the perimeter of the truck.

"I don't know about you, but I just got my Christmas present," she heard Cash say to someone, viewing the Christmas tree with pure satisfaction, as well as relief because they had managed to get this perfect specimen of a tree onto the flatbed without any incident.

"Yeah, me, too," she heard Ray agree softly, but when she looked up, she found that he wasn't looking at the tree. He was looking at her.

A very warm shiver danced down her spine.

Chapter Ten

Because the crew Miss Joan had brought with her to select this year's Christmas tree had found the one they wanted to put up in the town square rather quickly, they wound up returning to Forever well before dusk.

Word spread fast, and the town's citizens hurried over to the square to pass their own judgment on the Scotch pine.

As if she was leading a wagon train into the Wild West, Miss Joan brought her own truck to a stop in the center of town, jumped out of the cab and called for a halt of the other vehicles.

"We got another beauty," she announced to the sea of faces that surrounded her. A chorus of agreement met her statement.

Rather than just leave the tree where it was until the following day, Miss Joan decreed that there was enough daylight—and certainly enough willing hands—to get the tree off the flatbed truck and upright in the town square.

"You picked another winner," Harry proudly told his bride, planting a quick kiss on her cheek.

"Save that for later, Harry," she told him. "Right

now, I need harnesses and winches. You know the drill," she told her husband.

"Got 'em waiting right behind Mick's garage," Harry told her. He summoned a few men to come with him so that they could bring back the required equipment that would help the process of getting the tree upright and secured in the desired position.

Miss Joan relinquished control of this portion of the operation, allowing her husband to oversee it. Harry happily went to work, employing Cash and a number of the other younger men to get the job done. They worked in harmony, having either done this before or watched it being done year after year.

Ninety minutes after rolling into town with the giant Scotch pine, this year's Christmas tree was up, stable and secure—and ready to be decorated.

Everyone who wanted to, regardless of age, took part in this phase of the event. The only rule was to wait until the lights were put up, which they were in amazingly short order, thanks to the practically military precision instituted by Harry. Beyond that, once the lights were operational, there were no rules to follow other than to have fun.

There was no end to the number of people who wanted to be part of this segment of the ceremony—because it was such a beloved tradition.

Looking around the town square, Ray saw not just his father—who happen to be Harry's best friend and might have been in town for reasons other than the tree decorating ceremony—but his brothers and sister, as well. Granted Alma and Gabe both worked in town, but standing around in the square, waiting to be able to take their turn at adorning the Christmas tree, was not part of their normal job description.

Just as it wasn't part of Olivia Santiago's job description. Besides being the sheriff's wife, she was also one of the town's two lawyers, having formed a partnership with Alma's husband, Cash. Saturdays were either for catching up at the office or trying to cram in seven days of family life into two. But here she was, with everyone else. Right now, it was hard to say who was the more casually dressed, Olivia or her husband, both of whom were usually so carefully and formally attired.

Ray grinned as he scanned the area. Wearing what looked like their most comfortable clothes, everyone had come out for the occasion that was viewed by many as an unofficial day of celebration.

"You picked a really pretty tree, Holly."

Turning around to the source of the comment, Holly saw that even her mother had come out to join the rest of the town. Or, more accurately, Martha Johnson had been brought out by Ray's brother Eli. Eli and his wife, Kasey, followed by their two-year-old son, had steered Martha's wheelchair to the center of town to await the tree's arrival.

Martha, although exceedingly independent, appreciated the help since she had her hands full at the moment.

Holly saw that her niece, Molly, was comfortably seated on her mother's lap. Seeing Holly, however, the little girl wiggled off her grandmother's lap and made a mad dash for the woman she considered to be more mother than aunt. What she lacked in height she more than made up for with her boundless energy and enthusiasm.

"Holly, Holly, Holly!" the little girl cried with enthusiasm as she wrapped her arms around Holly's legs. "The tree is here!" she declared excitedly.

"I know, Monkey, I helped bring it in," Holly told the little girl with a laugh as she scooped her niece up in her arms. "I take it you like it."

"Very much," Molly answered with a sharp, smart nod of her head, sounding for all the world as if she was an old person trapped in a child's body instead of the age she really was.

"We'll leave you in good hands," Kasey murmured to Martha as Kasey and her husband withdrew along with their son.

"Thank you!" Martha called after the couple.

"Mom, what are you doing here?" Holly asked her mother as soon as she had her attention.

"Same thing everyone else is doing here—waiting to do my part in decorating the tree. Just because I can't get up on my tiptoes anymore doesn't mean I'm ready to be shipped off to the elephant's graveyard just yet. I've still got a chapter or two left in me."

"I know that, Mom, I didn't—" Holly began, only to be interrupted by her niece.

Older in spirit and mind than she was in actual years, Molly looked at her grandmother, a panicked expression crossing her face as she cried, "Don't go to the elephant's graveyard, Grandma. Please don't go. I don't want you to," she pleaded.

Laughing, Holly kissed the top of her niece's head. "Nobody's going anywhere, Monkey. Your grandmother's going to be around for a very long, long time. Okay?" she asked, looking into Molly's puckered face.

The little girl looked as if she was on the verge of crying at any second.

Then, just like that, the tears vanished.

Molly bobbed her head up and down with such force, Holly half expected it to pop off her neck. But Molly didn't even look dizzy.

Crisis averted, Holly picked up a shiny star ornament laid out on one of the tables that had been brought to the square. There were tables lining two sides of the square so that everyone could have access to the decorations.

"Okay, Monkey, let's see how high you can reach," Holly told her niece, presenting her with the ornament.

Molly examined the star, then, cocking her head, looked up at the towering tree. "You gonna hold me up?" she asked.

"That's cheating," Holly pretended to protest. Molly's small face instantly puckered up again and she looked upset.

"No, it's not. I'm a little girl. I can't reach high without you. Please, Holly?" she pleaded.

"Don't be a bully, Doll," Ray told her, joining the three generations that comprised his best friend's family. He looked down at the little girl. "Would you like me to hold you up, Molly?" he asked.

Molly had developed a king-size crush on Ray in the past month or so and she smiled from ear to ear at her heartthrob's suggestion. She put her arms out to him, wiggling to get free.

"Yes, please," she agreed with enthusiasm.

Because he was taller than Holly, Ray could hold the little girl up even higher in his arms—and for longer—than Holly could.

The latter ability became very necessary because, as it turned out, Molly had trouble making up her mind exactly where she wanted to hang the ornament. After changing her mind a total of three times, she finally settled on a branch.

Once it was hung and deemed secure on its perch, Ray was allowed to put her down. He did as he was instructed.

"Typical female, can't make up her mind," he said with a laugh.

"I'm not tip-ick-cal," Molly protested indignantly. "Grandma says I'm special."

"And special you are," Holly agreed, ruffling the little girl's hair. Holly turned toward her mother. "Mom, you want to hang up another ornament?" she asked, ready to fetch a second one for her from a nearby table. Her mother had already placed one on a low branch while waiting for Molly to hang hers.

But Martha demurred. She was here to observe and watch over her granddaughter. "No, I'm fine, dear. I just want to watch everyone else decorate the tree, if you don't mind," she said.

Holly didn't like her mother hanging back like this. It wasn't like her. Did that mean that something was wrong? Rather than asking—and receiving a negative answer, as she knew she would since her mother hated complaining—she took another approach.

"I don't mind," Holly told her mother. "But you have to hang at least one more ornament, Mom. Those are the rules, you know that. If you show up, you have to hang up," Holly said, quoting the rule Miss Joan was said to have made up years ago.

"Tell you what, Mrs. Johnson. You pick one out and I'll get you in close so you can hang it up a little higher," Ray offered cheerfully.

Martha nodded. "I'd like that, Ray."

"You do have a way with the Johnson women," Holly said to him, lowering her voice to a whisper.

He flashed a grin her way just as he guided her mother's wheelchair toward the tables where the decorations were laid out.

The tree wouldn't be fully decorated today, not by a long shot. It was never completely decorated within one day's time, and they were already working with an abbreviated day, but at least they had gotten a good head start on the job.

The town's tallest ladders—housed the rest of the year in Silas Malcolm's barn because it was the closest large space to the town square—had been put up against the tree so that, in addition to stringing up the lights, people could decorate the top portion of the tree.

Holly stood back and watched as people took turns—in some cases just once, in other cases as many turns as they could squeeze in—using the ladder and dressing the tree until evening finally blanketed the square, robbing it of much-needed light.

"That's it for today," Miss Joan announced as she called a halt. "We'll get started tomorrow just after first light," she said, more out of habit than necessity, since the rules were never changed.

And neither did the ritual that came next.

"All right, coffee and pie for everyone," she declared.

Hooking her arm through her husband's, she briskly led the way to the diner. The coffee was intended for all the participants who were fifteen and over. Those who had joined in and were younger received glasses of milk to wash down their servings of pie—or cookies, if they preferred.

"I love this time of year," Holly confided to her mother as she got behind the wheelchair, ready to push the woman to the diner, which was located only a few blocks away from the town square.

"So do I," Martha agreed, but her voice sounded a little weary to Holly. If she had any doubt, her mother's next words confirmed her thoughts. "Listen, I'm a little tired—and apparently Molly is even more so." Martha nodded at the little girl who was sleeping curled up on her lap. "We're going to go home."

"Okay," Holly said without a single word of protest, turning the wheelchair in the opposite direction.

"No, Holly, by 'we' I mean Molly and me, not you," her mother clarified. "I want you go on to the diner with the others."

She had no intention of letting her mother push herself all the way home. "That's okay, Mom, I—"

"No, it's not okay. I insist," Martha said firmly, cutting in. "And I know what's running through your mind," she added. "Don't you treat me like an invalid. I'm perfectly capable of taking my granddaughter home and putting her to bed. There's no need for you to cut your evening short just to hover over me," her mother informed her.

"Especially if she has help," Miguel Rodriguez

Sr. said, gently edging Holly out of the way as he took over the handles on the back of her mother's wheelchair.

Martha twisted around in her chair to look at this new champion she'd attracted. "Miguel, I don't need your help, either."

Ray's father nodded understandingly. "I know," he replied in his soft, accented voice. "But perhaps I need to do something gallant and this would be a very nice opportunity. Do not spoil it for me, Martha. Let me pretend to come to your rescue," he told her. "And this way, you can use both your arms to hold your granddaughter on your lap instead of trying to balance her and keep her from falling off as you go around corners, yes?"

Martha surrendered with a sigh. "If you insist."

"That I do," Miguel told her, then looked over his shoulder at Holly just before he began to push the wheelchair in the direction of the Johnson house. He winked at Holly, looking at that exact moment for all the world like his youngest son, Holly couldn't help thinking.

"Go, enjoy yourself a little bit," he encouraged her. "You do not do that nearly often enough—and you really should."

"He's right, you know," Ray said, putting his hands on her shoulders and physically turning her toward the diner. "You don't relax nearly often enough anymore. I can remember you had a lot more fun as a kid."

"Kids are supposed to have fun," Holly pointed out, but she was walking in the direction he'd steered her. "Adults are supposed to work."

"Okay, I'll give you that—in general. But nowhere is it written that work has to be twenty-four hours a day, every single day," he pointed out. "Even machines wear out like that."

Holly stopped walking and turned to face him for a moment. Did he forget?

"I took today off," she reminded him.

"No, you didn't," he contradicted. She opened her mouth to protest, but he talked right over her. "You didn't put in a full day at the diner—but you did work up a sweat," he pointed out. "That's work."

Holly shrugged away his comment. "There are lots of ways to work up a sweat that don't have anything to do with work."

The way he looked at her told Holly that he had attached a very particular meaning to her words, a meaning that she hadn't necessarily intended.

She could feel herself blushing again, damn him.

"Did you blush this much when we were younger?" Ray asked her teasingly. "I can't remember, but I don't think so."

Holly deliberately picked up her pace, walking fast so she could get ahead of him and he wouldn't be able to see her face.

"Hurry up, slowpoke," she urged. "Let's get going before all the pie is gone."

"As long as we get to the counter before Big Jim Zucoff claims a spot, we're okay," he told her, picking up his pace nonetheless. "That man'll eat anything that doesn't eat him first, and I've never seen anyone with a bigger sweet tooth than Big Jim."

"Miss Joan will keep an eye on him," Holly assured him. The other woman liked to keep things fair and equal, making sure that no one had an unfair advantage over anyone else, and Big Jim could eat faster than anyone she'd ever met. "Remember, she did last year."

"But he's bigger this year," Ray pointed out with a laugh. "I don't think anything'll succeed in reining him in, short of throwing lassos around him, tethering him and staking the ends of the lassos in the ground."

"Well, if anyone can do it, Miss Joan can," Holly bantered back, but her mind wasn't really on the man they were talking about, or the coffee and pie Miss Joan was giving away or even the Christmas tree she'd worked so hard to help bring back into town.

No matter what words came out of her mouth, Holly's mind was stuck in third gear and totally focused on those few precious moments when time had stood still and Ray's mouth had found hers again.

Except that this time, though she wouldn't have thought it was possible until she'd experienced it, had been even more intimate and stimulating than the first time that Ray had kissed her.

The way she saw it, there was nothing she could find under her tree come Christmas morning that could possibly come close to competing with what she'd already experienced.

As far as she was concerned, she'd already had her Christmas miracle—and it would last her for many Christmases to come.

Chapter Eleven

Sitting in front of her outdated computer, Holly felt her eyelids drooping. She struggled to keep her eyes open. But it was definitely not easy.

She'd gotten up early—as usual—to put in some study time. Exams were coming up soon and she needed to be ready for them if she was ever going to achieve her goal and become a nurse. However, getting up early, staying up late and working her study schedule around her workday as well as the needs of her mother and Molly was definitely challenging.

But then, she kept telling herself over and over again, if it wasn't challenging—if all this phenomenal amount of juggling were easy for her—then life would have been extremely boring with a capital *B*. It was in her nature to work hard, and she'd always *liked* challenges.

It was just a wee bit difficult to work *this* hard and be *this* challenged. Holly had to admit that she would have welcomed being a little less challenged once in a while.

"Damn it," she muttered under her breath. Her eyes had closed again. She had to stop doing that or she was going to flunk.

Unless, of course, she found a way to absorb all this information by osmosis.

Fat chance.

"Are you asleep at the computer again?"

Holly's eyes flew open as she heard her mother wheeling herself into the small bedroom that had been converted into Holly's study area. She'd thought that her mother was still in bed. Just how long had she been asleep anyway?

"Nope, not me," Holly denied cheerfully. She pressed her lips together to suppress the desire to yawn. "Just resting my eyes, that's all."

"Uh-huh," Martha murmured, clearly skeptical. "You should try resting the rest of yourself once in a while, as well." Her mother shook her head disapprovingly. "You go on burning the candle at both ends this way, one day you're going to find that you're not going to have any candle left. You know that, right?"

Holly closed down her computer. It was time for her to go to the diner and work.

"Sure I will, Mom." Holly turned from the darkening monitor and lightly brushed a kiss against her mother's cheek before she got up. "Now if you'll excuse me, I've got to get to work."

"Why don't you call in sick and go catch up on your sleep?" her mother suggested.

"Because Miss Joan doesn't pay me for being beautiful, Mom," Holly said, tongue in cheek. "She pays me for showing up and working."

Striding to the front of the house, Holly rummaged through the hall closet, found her jacket and put it on. The temperature had dropped in the past couple of days and it was actually rather chilly in the morning.

She supposed that since it was December, she really shouldn't be complaining. A lot of the country was dealing with record snow storms, so a little temperature drop was a small thing in comparison.

"She also doesn't pay you for being dead on your feet," Martha pointed out.

"Who's dead on her feet?" Holly asked, feigning confusion.

Martha frowned. "Don't play dumb, Holly. You could never pull that off. Even as a baby, you were always alert, always quick to look as if you understood what was going on."

"And you're not prejudiced in any way, right?" Holly laughed.

Martha lifted her chin as if she'd just been unfairly challenged. "Of course not."

Holly grinned. "Maybe you're giving just a little too much credit to a toddler, Mom—even if that toddler was me."

Martha sighed, throwing up her hands and resigning herself to business as usual as far as her daughter was concerned. "I don't know why I keep hitting my head against the wall like this. You never listen to anything I say anyway."

"Sure I listen, Mom. I just reserve the right to pick and choose which advice I want to follow and which I want to put away for another time," she answered tactfully. They both knew that the second kind of advice wasn't being put off for another time but being put away into cold storage, to be ignored for *all* time. "I'll be fine, Mom, really. Please stop worrying. I'll cut back on this hectic pace soon, I promise."

"Right, when you land in the hospital in Pine Ridge."

"Ever the optimist, Mom." Holly laughed, shaking her head.

"No, what I'm being is a realist, Holly. You simply can't keep going like this without some sort of consequences."

"And I won't keep going like this," Holly promised. She was going to be late, but she couldn't just leave when her mother was this upset with her. She needed to put her mother at ease as well as make her understand that right now she needed to keep up this pace a little longer. "I'll be graduating in less than six months—provided I pass my tests—and with any luck, new worlds will open up for me. For us," Holly amended, smiling warmly at her mother.

Martha appeared far from convinced. "If you haven't worked yourself to death by then."

"Never happen, I promise," Holly said, raising her right hand as if she were taking a solemn vow. "I won't let it."

Her mother murmured something under her breath about it not being all up to her, but Holly was determined to leave while she was still ahead in the game—or at least even. She dearly loved her mother, but Martha Johnson could talk a person to death once she got going on a subject. And right now, Holly thought, she had only so much energy to work with and it was all she could do to stay awake and functioning.

There was a whole day stretching out in front of her. If she spent time arguing with her mother, that would take up energy she needed for work, for studying tonight and for giving Molly a little quality one-on-one time, as well.

And what about you? When do you get some me *time?* a little voice in her head demanded.

The thing Holly had discovered about little voices was that she could ignore them if she chose. It was all mind over matter, properly applied.

"Hold down the fort until I get home, Mom." She kissed Martha's cheek again. "We'll talk about this then."

"No, we won't," Martha predicted as Holly left the house.

Right you are again, Mom.

Holly walked briskly to the diner. She passed the town square and the lovely Christmas tree, which now stood in all its finery like a giant, well-dressed sentry. All the decorations had been hung—if not all with the greatest of care, then at least with the greatest of affection.

She smiled to herself as she hurried by it. To her the tree was a symbol of the harmony that existed in Forever. She dearly loved living in a town that had traditions such as this one. From the bottom of her heart, Holly felt sorry for the people who were living in big cities, people who passed their neighbors on the street without a clue as to who they were or what kind of people they were.

Wax poetic later, Holly. If you don't pick up your pace, you're going to be late.

That's what she got for falling asleep in front of her computer, Holly berated herself. She was going to have to go over those last few pages she was supposed to have covered. Attempting to summon them now, she was drawing a blank. If those pages turned up on the exam, she was going to wind up failing it.

Shadows accompanied her through the streets, marking her path as she made her way to the diner. Dawn had yet to crease the horizon with the promise of first light.

Though she'd promised herself not to, Holly glanced at her watch. Five minutes after six. Not bad as far as being late went. Miss Joan was undoubtedly on the premises already. If it wasn't for the fact that she knew the woman lived with her husband in Harry's house, she would have sworn that Miss Joan slept in the diner so she could be there 24/7.

But when Holly arrived at the diner she found that the door was locked.

She looked at it in surprise.

Well, what do you know? She'd beaten Miss Joan in. That was definitely a first.

Holly fished out her key and unlocked the door. Miss Joan had given her her own key on the outside chance that she arrived first, but neither Miss Joan nor Holly had ever thought that was going to happen.

Holly caught herself hoping that everything was all right. Stripping off her jacket as she walked into the diner, she dropped it on the back of one of the chairs and went directly to the coffee urns. She had to get the first pots of coffee going.

She was filling the last urn with water for brewing tea when she heard the door to the diner opening behind her. Glancing over her shoulder in that direction, she saw Miss Joan in the doorway. The expression on the woman's face was somewhat bemused.

"You beat me in," she said.

Relieved that Miss Joan looked to be all right, Holly cheerfully replied, "Had to happen sometime."

"No, it didn't," the older woman retorted.

"Okay, I can leave and come back in again," Holly offered.

Miss Joan scowled at her as she deposited her purse behind the counter then shrugged out of her coat. "Don't patronize me, girl."

"I'm not patronizing you," Holly protested. "I'm just trying to guess what you want."

"Not even God can do that," Ray told her as he came into the diner himself.

Clearly not expecting anyone in this early, Miss Joan turned around and looked him over. "Well, look what the cat dragged in," she commented. "It's practically the middle of the night—at least for you. What are you doing out of bed so early, boy?"

Ray shrugged carelessly, as if he hadn't really noticed that he was the first customer at the diner, a fact he was acutely aware of.

"Thought I'd get an early start for a change," he told Miss Joan, carefully avoiding looking in Holly's direction—the old woman was a mind reader and he didn't want her thinking that he was here on account of Holly. He wouldn't even allow *himself* to think that. "Got a long list of things to do today."

"Like sitting on a counter stool, listening to your hair grow?" Miss Joan asked, tying on her apron. "Or are you here to watch my waitress work?" She gestured toward Holly.

"I'm here to have some of your excellent coffee and sample one of those fantastic raspberry-jelly donuts," Ray informed her.

Miss Joan laughed, shaking her head. "Well, I'll say one thing for you, boy. Your lies are getting smoother and rolling off your tongue with more charm. What do you think, Holly? Is Ray here becoming a more skillful liar than he used to be?"

Holly's early morning routine at the diner had become second nature to her and she could initiate it in her sleep—which some mornings was rather fortunate. But there was no sleepwalking through a morning that contained Ray. She was aware of every single movement she made—as well as every single one of his.

"I think he's just as attached to your jelly donuts and your coffee as he always is," Holly answered, waiting for her pulse to settle down to its normal irregular beat whenever Ray was anywhere around.

Miss Joan looked from one young person to the other. "You've been handling the donut orders for the past two years and as near as I can remember, you're the one who makes the initial pots of coffee in the morning, as well. Sounds to me like you're the one who should be garnering those compliments—or malarkey—from this boy and not me."

Ray sat down at the counter, taking the stool that was closest to where Holly was working. "Coffee ready yet?" he asked her, since as far as he could tell, the urn was still in the process of making its loud brewing noises.

"You're in luck," she told him. "The first urn just finished brewing." The other two urns were still going through their paces.

Holly poured the midnight-black liquid into a cup, placed it on a saucer and took it over to Ray. Setting the cup and saucer down on the counter, she selected a raspberry-jelly donut from the center of the box that had been delivered late last night and, placing that on a plate, put it beside the saucer on the counter. She put the creamer on the other side.

Within a moment, Ray had made short work of the cup of coffee. The rate he was consuming it made her think he needed it to wake up.

Ray exhaled, pure pleasure on his face as he looked her way. Two thirds of the coffee was gone when he set the cup back on the saucer. "Makes me feel like a new man," he declared.

"Nothing wrong with the old one," Holly heard herself saying before she could think her comment through and keep it to herself.

Surprised, Ray smiled at her while Miss Joan laughed shortly and said, "You're obviously not a very good judge of character, Holly. But you'll learn." Turning to Ray, she asked, "How's that wedding coming along?"

Startled, because his mind was clearly elsewhere, Ray looked at the woman with more than a little nervousness and asked, "What wedding?"

"Your brother Mike's wedding," Miss Joan specified, her eyes all but pinning him to the wall. "That's not off, is it?"

Of course she was talking about Mike's wedding. What other wedding would she have been referring to? Ray upbraided himself. Ever since he'd kissed Holly, his mind—not to mention other parts of him—had been playing tricks on him, making him wonder about things that he'd never wondered about or even contemplated before.

"No." And then he cleared his throat, repeating the word with more conviction. "No. As far as I know, it's still on."

"What else do you know?" Miss Joan asked with a strange, sly smile on her lips. A smile that made him fidget inside.

"About the wedding?" Ray asked, not sure if they were still on the same topic.

Miss Joan sighed and shook her head. "No, about how long panda bears live. Of course about the wedding. Are they still planning on inviting the whole town, or have they come to their senses and decided to elope?" She spared Holly a glance, saying, "Eloping is really the best way. Just you and your intended and the good Lord—and a preacher, of course."

Holly said nothing, but that definitely did sound good to her. Anything sounded good to her, as long as it included Ray.

Ray laughed at Miss Joan's suggestion. "Well, I know that Mike would probably like that idea a lot, but seeing as how Samantha doesn't really have any family to speak of, I think she kind of likes the idea of having a big wedding with lots of people around. And Mike likes seeing her happy, so yeah, they're still having the whole town at the wedding."

Pouring her own cup of coffee, Miss Joan leaned over the counter, fixed Ray with a very intense look and asked, "Anything else?"

He had no idea where Miss Joan was going with this—or even if the woman had a destination in mind. With Miss Joan, he'd learned a long time ago, nothing was what it seemed.

"Like what?" he asked innocently.

"Like are you part of the wedding party?" Holly asked, getting into the general inquisitive mood that seemed to be permeating the diner this morning.

"Me? Hell, no," Ray laughed, waving away the mere notion. "That would mean I'd have to put on a monkey suit."

"You could always go in that lovely outfit you have on," Miss Joan deadpanned, gesturing at the sheepskin jacket, plaid shirt and worn jeans that he was wearing.

But Holly had a serious question that she raised now. "You mean you wouldn't put up with a little discomfort in order to stand up for your own brother?"

Ray became somewhat defensive. "Hey, it's not like he's my only brother, and you wouldn't call it 'a little' discomfort if you'd had to put up with it like I did for the last wedding, when Rafe married Val. Or the one before that when Angel and Gabe did the same thing," he recalled.

Now that he'd gotten started, it was like opening up a floodgate. "Then there was Eli and Kasey. And Alma and Cash started the ball rolling when they got married." He'd been there for four of his siblings. That, as far as he was concerned, was above and beyond the call of duty. "Way I see it," he told her, "I've done my time."

"So you're bailing out on Mike?" Holly asked.

The way she said it sounded like an accusation, Ray thought. But rather than take offense, he just shrugged. "It's not like he'll miss me," Ray said glibly.

"The hell he won't," Holly countered. "I've seen all of you together. You all act tough, like you could take the rest of your family or leave it, but deep down, that's not true and you know it. You all love each other and there's not one of you who wouldn't go to their grave defending the others."

Ray stood up. "I've got to get going before you start charging me for this little head-shrink session," he quipped, digging into his pocket for money. Taking it out, he laid several bills on the counter.

"Keep it," Miss Joan said, pushing the money back at him. "It's on the house. You're going to need the money to rent that pretty little monkey suit you were just complaining about."

After a beat, Ray picked up the bills and shoved them back into his front pocket. "Thanks," he murmured.

Holly noticed that he didn't bother contradicting what Miss Joan had said. It looked as if Ray was going to be in another wedding party. Which meant that she had another opportunity to see him looking better than any man had an earthly right to be.

She didn't realize that she was smiling as she went about her work.

But Miss Joan did.

Chapter Twelve

As the diner door closed behind Ray, Miss Joan turned around to look at Holly. "Well, you seem to have things under control here, so I'm going to go over some of the order forms," the woman told her. "If you need me, I'll be in my office."

Holly nodded. She moved faster through her routine when she was alone. "Okay. I've got plenty to keep me busy out here."

She heard the front door opening again after what seemed like only a couple of minutes had passed. Holly didn't bother turning around when she asked, "Forget something?" She'd just assumed that Ray had doubled back to the diner for some reason.

She should have known it wasn't him when the hairs on the back of her neck didn't stand up the way they always did whenever he was in the vicinity.

"Yeah," a feminine voice said. "What my feet look like." The words were accompanied by a deep, heartfelt sigh.

Startled, Holly swung around to see Alma making her way to the counter at the pace of an arthritic snail. Holly glanced at her watch out of habit.

"You're early," she commented. The past couple of

months, Alma had taken to coming in every morning like clockwork for a large container of herbal tea to go. But she usually came in closer to nine, not seven.

"I know." Alma pressed her hand to her spine, no doubt trying to relieve an ever-present ache. "I thought if I showed up early at the sheriff's office, I could leave early, as well."

"To go home and put your feet up so you could get more comfortable?" Holly guessed, returning to the counter and rounding it in order to begin preparing the deputy's container of herbal tea.

Alma's laugh was short, harsh and dismissive. "Holly, I'm eight-and-a-half-months pregnant with a giant elephant—there *is* no comfortable position I can possible get to without first being knocked unconscious."

Holly gave her an understanding smile. "You have my sympathies. The usual?" she asked even as she got the pot of hot water.

"The usual," Alma echoed as she attempted to sit on a stool and redistribute her bulk in some sort of balanced fashion. But her eyes widened in distress before she could actually make satisfactory contact with the stool. "Speaking of usual," she said with a huge sigh, completely abandoning the notion of sitting. "Looks like I've got to pay a visit to yet another bathroom. I swear, I should just pick a bathroom stall and have all my mail forwarded there. It feels like I've got to go every three and a half minutes." She frowned at she looked down accusingly at her protruding abdomen. "Either this kid is spending all his or her time sitting on my bladder or my bladder has mysteriously shrunk down to the size of a pea."

"Maybe it's a little of both," Holly speculated helpfully. She'd picked up Alma's ambiguous reference to gender. "I take it that you still don't know what you're having?"

Alma shook her head. "I want to be surprised," she said as she began the slow journey to the rear of the diner where the restrooms were located.

"Well, you certainly have a lot more willpower than I do, Alma," Holly acknowledged. "If it were me, I'd want to know."

Alma flashed a weary smile in her direction. "I really like surprises." She winced a little. "Better make that an extralarge container, Holly. I need something to settle my stomach. I've been feeling really queasy since yesterday morning."

"Maybe you should go in to see the doctor," Holly suggested.

"I am, this afternoon. Right after my shift," Alma told her as she disappeared around the corner. "Until then, I need tea."

"One giant-size tea coming up, Deputy," Holly called out, reaching under the counter for one of the oversize cups that Miss Joan kept there.

Holly placed it on the counter, took two tea bags from the vacuum-packed canister where Miss Joan kept the herbal tea and deposited both into the cup. She then took it over to the urn and carefully poured the hot water over the tea bags.

While the tea bags were steeping, Holly went back to what she'd been doing to get the diner ready for the morning crowd that would begin arriving within the hour, looking to have breakfast.

Almost ten minutes had passed before she remembered to check on the tea.

When she did, Holly frowned. The tea was darker than the way Alma usually drank it. But then, she *had* asked for a larger container, so maybe she wouldn't mind that the tea was stronger, as well.

"Hope you like your herbal tea strong, Alma," Holly said, addressing the comment to the woman she assumed had stopped to look at something at the rear of the diner after she'd left the restroom. When she didn't receive even a grunt back, Holly glanced over her shoulder. "Where are you anyway?" she asked, half directing the question to the absent deputy, half to herself.

Maybe I should check on her, Holly thought, growing a little concerned.

Rounding the counter, she made her way to the rear of the diner, expecting to walk headlong into Alma at any moment.

But she reached the restroom door, and still no deputy.

Cocking her head, Holly paused for a second, listening to see if she heard any sort of movement on the other side of the door.

She didn't.

She was becoming uneasy. Alma was taking too long. Something wasn't right.

"Alma, are you in there?" Holly asked, raising her voice.

There was no answer.

Why?

She knew that Alma couldn't have left the diner without her noticing. There was only one way in or out, and the deputy would have had to pass the counter in order to leave. It wasn't as if there was a crowd she could have blended into.

Had she gone to see Miss Joan for some reason? Holly wondered. The woman was her mother-in-law and maybe there was something Alma wanted to share with Miss Joan.

But even as Holly came up with the excuse, it just didn't sit well with her.

Something was wrong, she could feel it in her bones.

"Alma?" she called through the door. "I'm coming in, okay?"

Very slowly, Holly pushed open the outer door with her fingertips, giving Alma every chance to call out and tell her to stay outside. When she didn't, Holly pushed the door open all the way.

That was when she saw her.

Alma was lying facedown on the floor. She appeared to be unconscious. Oh, God, had she fainted?

For a fleeting second, Holly thought of running for help, but she just couldn't move. Maybe she'd already allowed too much time to go by and this was one of those times where every second was critical. The thought all but froze her in place.

Rather than leave Alma, Holly shouted as loudly as she could, *"I need a little help in here!"*

Holly dropped to her knees beside the unconscious pregnant woman—which was when she realized that she was kneeling in something damp.

Alma's water had broken.

Her hand on Alma's shoulder, Holly tried to gently shake her awake.

"Alma? Alma can you hear me?" she asked urgently. "Alma, it's Holly. Can you tell me what happened?"

Since Alma was still lying facedown on the tiled floor, all she could make out was one eyelid fluttering slightly. It was enough to give her hope.

"That's it, Alma, wake up. You can do it. C'mon, try to sit up for me," she coaxed.

Angling, Holly slipped her arm under the older woman's shoulder—which was when she heard Alma's involuntary cry.

Alma's eyes flew open—and immediately filled with pain. "No, I can't… It's…the baby… The baby's…coming," she cried in an unnatural panic, each syllable sounding as if it was physically being wrenched out of her throat.

"I've got to get you to the doctor," Holly told her, doing her best not to panic herself. This was a natural process, a perfectly natural process, right? Women had been giving birth, with or without help, for centuries, right?

But when she tried to move Alma, the other woman clutched tightly on to her arm, trying to stop her from doing that.

"No, I can't… I *can't.*"

Holly regrouped. "Okay, you don't have to get up." She started to rise. "I'll go get him to come—"

Holly never got the chance to say *here*. Alma caught her wrist in what felt like an iron grip. "No… stay…*please,*" she pleaded. "Now… Coming… *Now!*" she cried between firmly clenched teeth.

Holly took a deep breath. This was *not* going well. "Okay, I'll stay, Alma. I'll stay," she promised. With effort, Holly centered herself. And drew on what she knew. She offered Alma an encouraging smile. "And don't worry, you're actually not my first. I brought Molly into the world."

For a second, she recalled the utter chaos of that night, with her brother yelling orders at her and his girlfriend crying and screaming. And there she'd been, caught up in the eye of the hurricane, praying she didn't mess anything up.

Molly had arrived in less than a heartbeat—and she was perfect.

"Jill went into labor three weeks early and there was no time to get her to the doctor, either. And I know more now than I knew then because of those nursing courses I've been taking, so everything's going to be all right. Trust me."

She was doing her best to put Alma at ease, but apparently she wasn't being too successful. Alma still looked scared.

"But, Alma, I'm going to need my hand," Holly told her gently. The words didn't seem to register with the pain-racked deputy. "Let go of my wrist, Alma," Holly requested a little more forcefully.

Belatedly, Alma opened up her hand, then instantly dug her fingertips into her own palms. The pain was almost making her pass out.

"Sorry…" Alma breathed.

"Nothing to be sorry about," Holly said soothingly. "I get it."

Stripping off her apron, Holly did her best to slide it under the deputy's writhing body. From this new position, Holly got a better look at Alma's face. There was a fresh cut, still bleeding, right above her right eye. It wasn't very hard to figure out what happened. Alma had to have hit her head on the edge of the sink when she fainted.

But right now, that was of secondary importance. Bringing this baby into the world, healthy and sound, was her first priority.

"This…is…*awful*…" Alma cried.

"It'll be over soon, I promise," Holly told her.

With determination, she folded back the bottom of Alma's oversize blouse and then tugged down the khaki-colored elastic-waist slacks she had on, taking them off the deputy.

"This is where it gets personal, Alma," Holly muttered. "But like I said, it'll be over with soon." *It just won't feel so soon until it's over,* she added silently.

One look told her that not only was the baby crowning, but that this baby was coming whether or not either one of them was ready for its arrival.

"Very soon," Holly told her.

"Holly?" Alma cried uncertainly.

Holly heard everything she needed to in Alma's voice. She knew what the deputy was asking her.

"The baby's coming, Alma. I need you to bear down and push," she instructed. "I'll do the catching." Alma screamed as a fresh pain ripped through her. The sound vibrated through Holly's head, all but making her deaf. "Well, you've certainly got that part down. Now *push!*" Holly ordered in a voice that would have made a drill sergeant envious.

The door directly behind her swung open just then. "I heard that all the way through the diner. What the hell is going on here— Oh, my God!" Miss Joan cried out as the sight of her daughter-in-law lying on the bathroom floor and what that meant registered. "Alma, baby, are you all right?"

"She's fine, Miss Joan," Holly told her, trying to keep her voice calm. "You're about to become a grandmother. If you're not busy," Holly added drolly, "could you get behind her, please, and support her shoulders?"

For one of the few times in her life, Miss Joan appeared indecisively torn. "I'll go run to get the doctor—"

"There's no time," Holly snapped impatiently, cutting Miss Joan short. "Get someone else to go. I need you to get down behind Alma, Miss Joan. *Now!*"

Without another word, Miss Joan did as she was told. Hurrying out, she called to the only other person in the diner, Angel, and dispatched her for the doctor. Rushing back into the bathroom, she knelt down directly behind her daughter-in-law and propped Alma's shoulders up against her own body before adding her hands to the effort. She pushed Alma into a forward position so that she could do as Holly instructed.

"Okay, Alma," Holly said, focusing entirely on the deputy. "Now push again. Harder."

"I...*am*...pushing...*harder.*"

"Again!" Holly ordered.

The next moment there was the sound of another voice, far higher, joining in.

Crying.

"It's a girl, it's a beautiful, beautiful baby girl! You have a girl, Alma," Miss Joan said, sobbing as she remained leaning forward, propping Alma up.

Holly, holding the brand-new life in her hands, offered the infant to her grandmother.

Miss Joan was shaking as she accepted the baby and wrapped her arms around it. "Perfect," she pronounced, never taking her eyes off the precious life she was holding.

Rocking back on her heels, Holly exhaled a ragged breath. That had been the most nerve-racking, exhilarating experience she'd had in a very long time. She recalled the thrill of holding Molly in her arms after coaching her transition from womb to world. It was a heady feeling.

She began to get up. "I'm going to go get a knife to cut the cord," she told Alma.

A feeling of déjà vu all but blanketed her when she felt Alma grabbing her by the wrist again, her eyes once more wide with pain that went on to etch itself on her face.

"Holly?" Alma cried, bewildered yet certain at the same time. "I'm not done yet. I'm having twins."

Rocking back on her heels again, Holly was about to ask her what she was talking about, but then the next second, there was no need. Back to her initial position on the floor beside Alma, she saw that there was another head pushing forward, struggling to come into the world.

Twins?

"What's going on?" Miss Joan cried, looking from Alma to Holly. Given where she was, sitting directly behind Alma's head, the older woman didn't see what was happening.

"Cash and I didn't tell anyone. We…wanted to… keep…it our…secret…"

"You really do like surprises, don't you?" Holly marveled, looking at Alma. "Okay, here comes number two!" she announced, hunkering down. "You know the drill, Alma. Push!"

Alma did as she was told. She pushed.

Holly offered what encouragement she could, urging Alma to push at regular intervals. After enduring what felt like the longest minutes of her life, Holly found herself helping ease Miss Joan's *second* grandchild out into the world.

Alma's scream was almost muted in comparison to the scream that had initially brought Miss Joan running to the restroom.

Holly held the second baby close to her. The warmth that worked its way all through her had little to do with the infant's body temperature.

"It's a boy, Alma," she said, looking at the worn-out, brand-new mother. "You got one of each." As gently as possible, she laid the second infant in Alma's arms. "No offense, Alma, but I sure hope that you're finally closed for business now," she said, nervously eying Alma's lower half.

This time, there was no explosive follow-up.

For a second time, Holly started to rise to her feet. Unlike the first time, she made it.

"I'm going to get some clean dish towels to wrap around these babies," she told Miss Joan and Alma.

She sincerely doubted that either woman heard her. But that was okay, as they were otherwise occupied, Holly thought, smiling to herself as she stepped out of the restroom—

And right into Ray.

"What the hell happened to you?" he asked, staring appalled at the state of the front of her uniform.

For the first time since she had met him, her Raydar, as she secretly referred to her ability to feel his presence wherever he was, had failed to go off and alert her to the fact that Ray was around.

Collecting herself, she stepped back.

"I just got a frantic call from Cash saying that Alma wasn't answering her cell phone and the sheriff said she should have been there half an hour ago. I know she picks up her tea here first so I thought I'd ask if you'd seen her."

The words came out in a rush as he went on staring at the blood on her uniform.

Holly nodded numbly. "Alma's in the ladies' room at the moment."

Sensing the blood he was looking at wasn't Holly's, he asked, "Is she okay?"

Holly took a deep breath, trying to center herself and calm down. "She is now. Oh, by the way, congratulations." Her eyes crinkled as she grinned at him. "You're an uncle."

As far as he knew, Alma wasn't due for another couple of weeks. The doctor had calculated that the baby was to arrive right after Christmas. He stared at Holly blankly. "What?"

"Alma just had her baby," she enunciated slowly, then corrected herself. "Her babies."

Ray was still working his way through the first part of the sentence. "Here?" he cried.

She nodded. Opening a drawer located off to the side, she took out several fresh towels. "They couldn't wait."

"Wait— What? They?" Ray repeated, clearly confused. He stared at Holly, trying to decide which of them had lost their minds. "What do you mean they couldn't wait? Who's they?"

"They are your new nephew and niece. Alma gave birth to twins," she told Ray. "Seems that she and Cash were holding out on us. Apparently, only they and the doctor knew. Speaking of which, where is he?" she wondered out loud. "Miss Joan sent someone to go get him."

Meanwhile, Ray was apparently not listening. He'd stopped at the mention of the word *twins*. She'd never seen Ray turn pale before.

Chapter Thirteen

"Twins?" Ray repeated. "Two babies?" He stared at her as if she'd just told him that aliens from Mars had landed. "Are you sure?"

It was amazing what men decided to question. Didn't he think she could count?

"I brought them into the world one at a time, so yes, I'm sure. What would you call two babies born a few minutes apart?"

"A shock," Ray answered automatically. "Oh, my God, Cash doesn't know she gave birth already, does he?"

"Not unless there's a spy camera inside the ladies' room. Can you go get him?" she asked. "And see what's keeping Dr. Davenport, too," she added. "I'd go myself but I'm a little bushed right now," Holly confessed.

"I'm an idiot," Ray suddenly realized, saying the words by way of an apology. He'd been so stunned by the information she'd given him and so concerned about his sister, he'd completely ignored the fact that Holly had been there for Alma when his sister had needed someone the most. "Can I get you anything?" he asked, glancing around to see what he *could* get for her. His familiarity with the diner ended on the other side of the counter.

Ray's question surprised her. And touched her. She waved away his offer even as she secretly held it close to her heart.

Most likely, Ray probably didn't know how sweet he was being, she thought. But that was okay. She knew, and that was all that mattered.

"No, I'm okay," she told him. "Alma did all the work. I just coached her. But if you could get the doctor and Cash here, that would really go a long way to ensuring Alma's well-being on all fronts. She looks healthy enough, but hearing Dr. Davenport say so will make all concerned happy."

Ray nodded and was halfway to the door when he suddenly spun around on his boot heel and doubled back to her.

Surprised, she looked at him uncertainly. "Something wrong?"

"Nope, not a thing." And then he grabbed her by the shoulders and planted a very enthusiastic kiss on her lips. "You're the best!" he declared with equal enthusiasm.

Then he released her shoulders and made it through the diner's front door in less than two thuds of her accelerated heart.

If her knees hadn't felt weak before, they certainly did now.

But, before, it was all due to tension. Granted she knew what she was doing and, thanks to her studies, and because of Molly, she had more experience than the average person when it came to helping a woman through the painful process of giving birth.

But there was always the danger of something going wrong, some unforeseen element throwing the equation out of kilter.

In contrast, her knees now had the strength of overcooked spaghetti because Ray had just kissed her and told her she was the best.

She knew the reason any of it had happened was because Ray was both relieved that his sister was all right and grateful that she'd been there for Alma and hadn't just gone to pieces the way someone else might have—especially when confronted with the need to deliver two babies, not just one.

But whatever the reason, he'd kissed her and said those magical words. Words that made her feel absolutely special, if only for a few fleeting moments.

"You forget where the linens are, girl?" Miss Joan asked, suddenly appearing next to her. Startled, still embedded in her temporary euphoria, Holly gasped in surprise. Dropping her tough-as-nails facade, Miss Joan asked in concern, "Are you all right? You've been gone long enough to have gone to the emporium for those fresh towels."

"I'm fine," Holly was quick to assure her, then explained why she hadn't come back. "Ray was just here, looking for Alma. I sent him to get Cash and see what happened to the doctor."

"Good thinking. I'll go get those towels, you go keep that crowd in the restroom company," Miss Joan said, nodding toward the rear of the diner.

Holly waved the other woman back. "No, I got this. You just go back to Alma and visit with your grandbabies."

She expected Miss Joan to turn on her heel and return to the restroom, but instead, the woman looked at her and in an unexpected moment of tenderness, Miss Joan brushed a kiss on her cheek.

When Holly looked at her, stunned, she murmured, "Thank you."

Holly shrugged self-consciously. "Like just I told Ray, Alma did all the work."

"But you got her through it," Miss Joan pointed out. The next moment, she turned on her rubber-soled heel and disappeared around the corner, heading toward the restroom.

As if coming out of a trance, Holly snapped to it. She rushed off to the linen closet to finally get the fresh towels she'd come out for.

A minute later, Cash, looking far more stressed than she had ever seen him, came sprinting in like a man trying to outrun a cattle stampede. Seeing Holly, he cried, "Where?"

"Restroom," was all she said, pointing.

Cash had no sooner disappeared into the back to greet his new family than Ray and Angel returned with the town's only physician.

"Sorry," Dan apologized. "I was setting Zack Riley's broken arm and I couldn't just leave him. I've got to get another doctor out here with me," he told Holly wearily. "So where's my patient? Or should I say patients?" Dan asked, glancing around.

"Alma and the babies are in the restroom. So are Cash and Miss Joan."

"Looks like I'll need a shoehorn," the doctor commented as he began to make his way to the back, as well.

"Doc?" Holly called after him. When he stopped

and looked at her over his shoulder, waiting for her to continue, Holly held out the towels she'd fetched. "You might want to take these in with you. I've got the twins wrapped up in aprons right now."

Dan took the towels from her. There was admiration in his eyes as he said, "You are one resourceful young lady, Holly Johnson."

Again she shrugged, as if to physically deflect the compliment. She was accustomed to hanging back, to being in the background, not being noticed for any outstanding reason. "You just learn to make do in an emergency," she said by way of diminishing her accomplishment.

Because there were no noises coming from the back of the diner, Dan allowed himself to pause for a moment longer. "Ray told me you're studying to be a nurse and that you'll be finished with your courses within six months. Is that true?"

She was surprised that Ray had paid that much attention to what she'd told him. Usually their conversations were either about him, or the new woman who had caught his fancy. On those rare occasions when the conversation turned to her, she just assumed what she said went in one proverbial ear and out the other, scarcely registering.

"That's right," she replied, refusing to let her imagination go.

Dan smiled. It looked as if he was finally going to have a little help. "You can put this down under interning. I'll be happy to write a letter for you, and if you need more in the way of hands-on experience to graduate, come see me later and we'll arrange something. I could certainly use a good nurse in my practice."

It was Holly's turn to stare. She would have pinched herself, but she didn't want to run the risk of being woken up.

"I will," she told him, feeling as if she'd suddenly been completely recharged and could go on for hours.

Ray flashed her a grin and gave her a thumbs-up sign as he followed the doctor to the restroom.

If she thought she would have more time to dwell on and possibly savor this new development in her life, she realized she was mistaken. Behind her, she heard the noise of people walking into the diner. Hungry people who started their long days by having breakfast at Miss Joan's diner.

Turning around, Holly scanned the incoming faces, looking for either Angel or Eduardo, Miss Joan's short-order cooks. Energized or not, Holly knew she wasn't going to be able to take down orders and serve the customers after first cooking those same orders.

When she saw Eduardo coming in, Holly all but grabbed him and pulled the thin man toward the kitchen. "Oh, thank God."

The silver-haired cook, who had been verbally sparring with Miss Joan for as long as anyone could remember, looked at Holly and laughed.

"I have had many women say that when they saw me, but I am afraid that you are a little too young for my tastes, *chica*."

"And you're too young for mine," Holly countered, getting a second laugh out of the man. "But we're really shorthanded this morning and I need you to man the kitchen."

"Do I not always?" he asked, going behind the counter and opening the swinging door to the kitchen. "By the way, where is our grumpy boss?" he asked, looking around.

For now, she thought that keeping quiet about what had transpired in the restroom was for the best, so she said evasively, "In the back. She's busy. It's just you and me running things right now."

"Ah." He nodded his head knowingly, pleasure highlighting his features. "Good," he declared with a wink, then disappeared into the kitchen.

Squaring her shoulders and bracing for a long day, Holly went to take the order of the table at the far end of the diner.

HOLLY BEGAN TO feel as if the day was just never going to end.

Miss Joan eventually came out to help in the diner, once Alma and the twins—over Alma's protest— were taken to Pine Ridge to be thoroughly checked out.

Knowing that, despite Miss Joan's nonchalant act, the woman was concerned about Alma and the babies' well-being, Holly told the older woman that she was free to go along with her daughter-in-law. Not surprisingly, Miss Joan waved away the words.

"They need a little alone time right now—although alone time is what got them into this mess," Miss Joan commented, smiling to herself. Taking a deep breath, she took a slow look around the diner. "I see you're holding down the fort pretty well."

"Didn't have much of a choice," Holly told her, rushing by with three orders of pancakes and juice. "And besides, Eduardo's here to help, so it's not as bad as it could be." If she'd had to cook as well, everything might have come to a grinding halt indefinitely.

"Where's Laurie?" Miss Joan asked, scanning the diner a second time. Laurie was the other waitress on this morning shift.

Holly looked away as she answered, "She phoned in to say she was going to be late."

Miss Joan looked at her closely. "She didn't call, did she?"

Holly frowned. The only thing she hated more than lying was being caught lying.

"No," she admitted, "but Laurie'll be here. She always is."

"Let me give you a very important little life-saving tip," Miss Joan said, pausing to put an arm around her shoulders, forcing her to stop moving for a moment. "Don't ever play poker, girl. You have a really lousy poker face."

Still holding a full tray, Holly nodded. "I'll try to remember that," she said wryly. "Right now though, I'm busy trying to remember who gets what at table number four."

"Doesn't matter. That cocky little guy with the silver moustache back there can cook up boots nice and tender—and if you ever tell him I said so, you're fired, got that?" Miss Joan asked, giving Holly a look that penetrated clear down to her bones.

"Got it," she assured Miss Joan.

"Okay, then," Miss Joan said, releasing her again. "Get back to work."

"That was my intent, Miss Joan. That was my intent," Holly murmured under her breath, hurrying over to table four.

IT FELT AS if she'd been going nonstop and full steam ahead all day long. Added to that, in the middle of it all, Miss Joan had suddenly left her in charge and taken off with Harry to visit Alma at the Pine Ridge hospital.

It had been decided by all involved that Alma deserved to spend a night in the comfort of a hospital bed, being looked after and cared for before she began the hectic existence of being the mother of twins, which, some had already hinted, was like being thrown headfirst into roaring rapids.

After calling her mother to tell her to put Molly to bed because she wouldn't be home for several more hours, Holly stayed on for the third shift as well as her own first two.

Holly's extra shot of adrenaline was completely depleted by the time she finally closed up for the night. Dragging one foot after the other, it was all she could do to walk to the door, flip the switches and lock up. But once it was done, she breathed a sigh of relief.

Just as she turned away from the locked door, she heard someone knocking. Part of her felt like pretending she hadn't heard a thing and just keep going until she reached the back office.

But it was against her nature to turn her back on anyone. So, despite the fact that the other waitresses, as well as Angel and Eduardo, had left and she was all alone in the diner, Holly turned around to head back to the front door. Prepared to let in this night owl, she was going to warn him—or her—that all that was available was half a pie and the last of the coffee.

When she saw Ray standing on the other side of the door, her pulse accelerated as it always did, but not for the usual reason. Ray had been gone for most of the day, visiting at the hospital along with the rest of his family. Seeing him here could only mean one thing, Holly thought.

"Something wrong with Alma or the babies?" Holly asked breathlessly as she threw open the door to let him in.

He looked at her a little oddly as he walked in. "Not that I know of. Why?"

She stared at him, stumped. "Then what are you doing here?"

He laughed. "I thought that maybe the woman of the hour might like a ride home. Near as I can figure it, you've been going nonstop since about six this morning."

"Five," Holly corrected. "I've been up since five." God, but that seemed like a lifetime ago. "But then, who's counting?" she cracked. She stopped moving and stared at him again, as stunned now as she had been a second ago when she'd first heard him tell her why he was here. "You really came to give me a lift?" *Not that you don't do that every time you turn up near me,* she added silently.

"Sure," he said expansively. "Why not? You're my best friend," he reminded her. "And you went over and above the call of best-friend-dom today," he added with a wide grin. "So I thought that maybe I'd do something nice for you for a change."

As she sighed, she allowed herself to relax for a

moment and feel the full weight of her exhaustion. It seemed endless.

"I do appreciate your offer," she told him. "Because now that I've stopped moving, I feel just about wiped out," she confessed. But even though he said he was just doing payback, Holly felt she needed to offer him something in exchange for his being so thoughtful. "Would you like to have some dessert and coffee?" she asked, nodding toward the chocolate-cream pie that was still on display.

Ray nodded with enthusiasm. "Pie and coffee would be great—as long as you join me."

Holly was about to demur out of habit, then thought better of it. After all, it *was* after-hours. "Sure. But give me a minute."

Then, as he watched, she moved around the diner, turning off the lights in one area after another except for the light near the rear of the diner, which was completely out of view of the front door.

"What are you doing?" he asked. If he didn't know better, he would have said that she was setting a romantic scene rather than apparently locking up for the night.

"The diner's closed for the night, so if anyone looks in, I don't want them seeing the lights on. It might make them think that it's still open. They'll knock harder, expecting a response, and I'll feel guilty about not letting them in. It's a lot easier if I just turn off all the lights except that last one," she said, nodding toward the table in the far corner.

He laughed. It was all just so typically Holly. "That sounds like you, all right." He rounded the counter, going to the coffee urn. "Tell you what, let's have a division of labor. You get the lights, I'll get the pie and coffee," he offered.

"That's okay, I can—" But Holly didn't get a chance to finish.

"Don't argue," he told her, interrupting her protest. "It's about time someone served you for a change."

She had no idea how to answer that.

So she didn't.

Chapter Fourteen

"How's Alma?" she asked once she'd joined Ray at the table. She knew that he'd gone earlier today, along with the rest of his family, to Pine Ridge Memorial Hospital, to see his sister and the new twins.

Aside from wanting to know how things were going for the brand-new mother, Holly was also desperately trying to keep her mind on something other than the fact that the diner had suddenly become a very romantic-looking place, what with all the lights out except the one close to the table she and Ray were occupying.

The only way it could have been even more so was if there had been candles in place of the overhead light. And that would have completely spelled her doom.

"Restless," Ray answered. "You know Alma, she has trouble taking it easy, but she's fine," he told her, then added, "thanks to you."

Holly shifted. Maybe coffee and pie was a bad idea. All sorts of thoughts were crowding her head, none of which had anything to do with the immediate conversation and everything to do with the man she was having it with. "I already told you, Alma did—"

Ray rolled his eyes. "Will you learn how to take a damn compliment, already?" he said, raising his voice as he cut her off. "Nobody's going to think you're getting a swelled head or an inflated ego if you just say thank-you when someone says something positive about what you did."

Holly blew out a breath, then surrendered and murmured a small, "Thank you."

The corners of Ray's mouth curved as satisfaction entered his light brown eyes. "There. Was that so hard?" he asked.

Was it her imagination, or had the space between them at the table somehow gotten smaller? It had definitely grown more intimate.

"No, but—"

"Uh-uh-uh." Ray wagged a finger at her, deliberately calling a halt to anything further she might want to say. "I want you to quit while you're ahead." His whole family wanted to thank Holly, and he wasn't about to let her just dismiss what she'd done for Alma. "Besides, Alma told us that she'd felt faint, and from that gash on her forehead, I'm guessing she must have hit her head on the rim of the sink when she went down. If you hadn't found her, who knows how long she would have been out?"

Granted, she'd shaken Alma awake, but there was no way the woman would have remained unconscious for long. "Most likely until the first really strong contraction seized her, would be my guess," she told him.

It was his turn to shrug off a comment. Holly was just too damn modest for her own good, he thought. In this one area, she was the complete opposite of him. He liked to grab attention; she was apparently happier in the shadows. They could each stand to learn from each other, he decided—especially he from her—although he had no intention of admitting that. At least, not right now.

"All I know is that Alma said she wouldn't have gotten through it as well as she did if you hadn't been there for her. By the way," he threw in nonchalantly between forkfuls of pie, "Alma and Cash would like you to be the twins' godmother."

Holly dropped her fork to her plate as she stared at Ray, for once not undone by the heart-melting handsomeness she saw there but by what he'd just told her.

"What?"

"Godmother," he repeated slowly, enunciating each syllable. "You're not familiar with the concept of godmother?" he asked, tongue in cheek.

"No, of course I am," she retorted. "It's just that— wouldn't she want someone who's closer to her to be the twins' godmother?"

"Right now," Ray said, laughing, "the only being closer than you is God. My dad wants to adopt you. And Cash asked me to tell you that he'll be your attorney for life—for free. According to Alma—and Miss Joan—you stayed calm and collected throughout the whole process, from start to finish." Then he added, "That went a long way in calming Alma down."

He was looking at her strangely, Holly thought. Now what? Was there something he wasn't telling her? Her mind scrambled around, attempting to discover an answer. She came up empty.

"What?" she asked him.

He hadn't been aware that he was staring at her. He supposed that he was.

"I'm just impressed, that's all. I still kind of think of you as that skinny little kid I went swimming with at the lake every summer." And then he grinned at her. *Really* grinned.

She couldn't take her eyes off Ray. When he grinned like that, it went straight to the very core of her. Something was up. Something that went beyond her helping Alma give birth.

"Now what?" she breathed.

"I just remembered," he answered mysteriously.

It was like pulling teeth with this man. "Remembered what?"

The grin was turning downright sexy and just winding itself all through her system. She found it increasingly difficult to sit still and not fidget.

"That a few of the earlier times," he told her, "we went skinny-dipping."

"We were eight and nine," she reminded him. "There weren't any differences back then." At least, none that she'd felt self-conscious about. Exactly.

"Oh, there were differences, all right," he countered, a sexy, mischievous look entering his eyes.

She drew herself up, trying her best to look indignant and knowing that she couldn't quite pull it off. "You're just saying that to get under my skin and embarrass me." But she could hold out only so long. "You noticed?" she asked in a hushed whisper. As clearly as she could remember, they were just eager to get into the water and cool off.

"As I recall, I was a red-blooded little boy." He nodded. "I noticed." Ray saw the color spreading through her cheeks at an amazing rate. "You're going to blush now? Fifteen years after the fact?" he asked incredulously.

Really embarrassed now, Holly shrugged, looking away. "I didn't think you noticed," she mumbled.

"If I didn't, I should have," Ray told her, finally coming clean.

"Then you *didn't* notice," she concluded. A sigh of relief escaped her.

"Maybe not," Ray conceded. It wasn't his intention to embarrass her over something so far in the past. However, the present was a different matter. He'd have to be blind not to notice her attributes now.

How was it that he hadn't noticed until that evening he'd picked her up to go to Murphy's?

His eyes swept over her, lingering on the tempting swell of her breasts as she struggled to regulate her breathing.

"But I'm noticing now," he told her quietly.

She could have sworn his very words were dancing along her skin, making her feel unseasonably warm. Had the air shut down in the diner when the lights had been turned off? She couldn't tell.

"Maybe it escaped your notice, but we're not exactly skinny-dipping at the moment," she pointed out, congratulating herself for getting the words out when her throat and tongue were drier than the Texas Panhandle in the middle of a July heat wave.

"But we could be," he told her. "We're not too far from the lake."

"It's the middle of December," she said. Nobody thought about swimming in the lake in December.

"Water stays warmer than the land," Ray reminded her, his eyes never leaving hers.

Why hadn't he ever noticed before now just how really beautiful she was? Or had she gradually become that way, right under his nose, without his having been aware of her subtle metamorphosis?

He wasn't sure. All he knew was that he was noticing all that now, and it was hitting him where he lived, twisting his gut so that he could hardly catch a decent breath.

"I'm too tired to go skinny-dipping in the lake," she told him. Besides, the last thing she wanted was to come off like some desperate, clingy female, eager to take any crumbs he was willing to toss her.

"Rain check, then," he replied so seductively, it was really hard for her to concentrate.

Holly was barely aware of nodding her head. "Rain check," she echoed, feeling light-headed again and disconnected from the rest of herself.

She forced her mind to focus on her surroundings, on conducting herself as if it was business as usual with Ray, and what was usual was that his attention was *never* focused on her.

But it was now.

Holly looked down at his plate and saw that he had eaten the slice of pie she'd served him. Automatic pilot kicked in, causing her to ask, "Would you like to have another slice of pie?"

His eyes remaining on hers, Ray moved his head slowly from side to side. Then, just before he reinforced his reply verbally, he reached across the table and took her hand, stopping her as she began to rise.

"No," he answered, "I don't want more pie."

Why did that sound like a leading line? And why was she having trouble breathing, as if the very air in her lungs had turned solid and she couldn't draw in any more air to sustain herself?

Don't say it, don't say it, Holly cautioned herself. It would just be setting herself up for a fall.

And yet, despite her self-warnings, she heard the words coming out of her mouth.

"Then what do you want?"

He rose then and for a split second, she thought he was going to leave.

But he didn't.

Instead, he took her hand in his and silently coaxed her to her feet. Holly rose from her chair like someone caught in a trance, never taking her eyes away from him. Her heart began pounding so hard, she was surprised that she even heard him when Ray softly responded, "You."

She swallowed, doing her best to unglue the words from the roof of her mouth. "I'm not on the menu," she finally said through lips that were barely moving.

Ray smiled then, smiled right into her eyes as he said, "Good, because I like ordering things that are off the regular menu."

A shiver shimmied up her back, then down again.

It made no sense, and yet, somehow, it did.

But she had no time to try to puzzle it out because the very next moment, Ray had framed her face between his hands and brought his mouth down to hers so softly at first, that she thought she was fantasizing, creating the scenario by allowing her mind to drift right into a vivid daydream.

And as her blood began to heat in her veins, the warmth of his lips penetrated her very being, making her head spin as wildly as if she was on a merry-go-round. She knew what she was experiencing was real. Moved by gratitude or opportunity or just reacting to happenstance, Ray was kissing her. Kissing her and simultaneously unraveling life as she knew it.

Going with the moment, she leaned into him, into the hard outline of his body as she wrapped her arms around his neck and gave herself up to the wild sensation roaring through her.

And the more she did so—the more she did so. Each step, each moment, led to another and another.

This, she was certain, would only happen once, and then Ray would come to his senses, apologize and they'd never talk about it again. She knew that as well as she knew her name—but she didn't care.

All she cared about, all she wanted, was to have this one time, to allow it to turn into a memory that she could revisit again and again when she was feeling lost or alone, just so that she could experience the indescribable surge she was feeling right at this moment.

Holly groaned when his hands skimmed along the sides of her body, melted as his kiss deepened and then moaned when his lips trailed along the sides of her neck, weaving an array of soft, sensual kisses along every part of her that he came in contact with.

She could feel her very core quickening, yearning for his touch, for the union, however brief, that would forever have her belonging to him, no matter where life took either one of them. From this evening forward, she would indelibly be his.

Without being completely conscious of her actions, Holly began tugging at his shirt, her fingers nimbly working the buttons free from their confines, all the while kissing him with as much passion as she was receiving.

Engulfed in a heated haze, Holly felt him coaxing her back, guiding her out of the dining area and toward the rear of the diner, toward the one place that contained an overstuffed sofa.

The office where she did her inventory, where Tina Davenport, the doctor's wife, worked on the accounts and out of which Miss Joan ran the whole business.

Holly knew they shouldn't be in here. And they definitely shouldn't be doing what they were doing in here, but as she undid his belt buckle and pulled his belt free of the loops on his jeans, she knew that this time, decorum was *not* what she was after. Before something happened to call a halt to it, she wanted to have Ray make love with her once, just once.

And after thinking it was never going to happen, that he would always be chasing other women and never her, it was finally, finally happening.

HE WANTED HER.

She was breaking down his resistance as if it was constructed out of wet tissue paper, crumbling apart on contact.

Not that he had much resistance. He never really had, at least, not when it came to the fairer sex. But this was Holly. Holly, his friend, his pal, the keeper of his secrets…and, he just now realized, all this time she'd had a big secret she'd never even hinted at, never shared with him.

He had never guessed that there was a hot, smoldering woman just beneath the calm, precise surface. A woman he would never have *dreamed* existed.

But she did exist. And he found her exciting beyond words.

One thing was leading to another as if by some unseen design, and before he knew it, Ray realized that he'd removed the light blue uniform he had grown so accustomed to seeing Holly in. As it dropped to the floor, it unveiled a body that both stimulated him and, in a strange way, humbled him.

"You're right," he whispered against Holly's ear, as he brushed more ardent kisses along her skin. "You *have* changed since we went skinny-dipping. Changed a great deal."

The tone of his voice brought joy rushing through her heart to a degree she hadn't thought remotely possible. If she'd loved him before, she was insanely *in* love with him now.

Rather than answer or say anything at all, she began to kiss him with the passion she had tried to hold back, the passion she'd struggled to restrain all these years whenever she talked with him.

There was no holding back anymore because, as his hand brushed along the more sensitive places on her body, eruptions began to happen, one after the other, one feeding into the next until she thought she'd just die from the exquisite ecstasy of it all.

Twisting and turning into his touch, wanting more, not certain if she could really *withstand* more, Holly opened the eyes that she hadn't realized until this moment she'd closed and whispered with effort, "Make love with me, Ray. Make love with me *now.*"

His grin went straight to her heart as he pushed her back onto the sofa. "I thought that was what I was doing," he said in a teasing voice.

But his eyes were serious as he loomed over her. Balancing his weight on elbows that framed either side of her on the narrow sofa, Ray drew his hardened torso along her damp body, first lowering his mouth onto hers, then lowering his body, sealing it to hers as he entered her.

The brief moment of resistance he found there had him stunned. His first inclination was to draw back, and he would have had she not wrapped her legs around him and held him in place.

It forced him to go forward rather than retreat.

And then, there was no place for thought, no place for hesitation or noble efforts. There was just the all-consuming flame of desire.

Responding to the way she moved beneath him, he undertook an ever-increasing tempo, his hips prompting hers to go faster, faster, until he was all but panting as they raced up to the very top of the peak.

The magnificent release engulfed him.

He didn't even feel pain when Holly bit down on his lip in response to the wild surge that coursed through her veins.

And as he descended, his pulse continued to beat erratically. It took a while for his head to stop spinning.

And throughout it all, he held Holly close to him, afraid she might disappear if he didn't, even as disbelief at what had just transpired echoed through his brain.

Chapter Fifteen

Euphoria still had a very tight hold on her as Holly's pulse hit a more rhythmic, steady beat.

But despite the incredible, lighter-than-air euphoria, reality was beginning to elbow its way into her consciousness.

And reality was tightly bonded to fear.

Fear of the future, of what lay ahead as far as her friendship with Ray was concerned.

They had never been members of the "friends with benefits" club, at least not in the standard manner. The benefits that could be garnered by having her for a friend were that she would go to the limit and beyond in any capacity that was necessary *when* it was necessary, strictly to help him, with no thought to her own well-being.

This, however, wasn't part of that package or even remotely implied as a "benefit." Much as making love with Ray had thrilled her, she was terrified that the very act had brought irreversible consequences with it. Consequences that would ultimately spell the loss of his friendship.

Trying to blot all of that from her mind for just a little longer, Holly curled up against him, treasuring the warmth radiating from his body to hers. She gloried in the sound of Ray's heart beating not quite calmly beneath her cheek. She wished with all her heart she could find a way to just freeze time, to make it stand still at this moment indefinitely. This was the absolute perfect high point of her life. It was not going to get any better than this, and most likely, Holly felt, it would only go downhill from here.

"You didn't tell me." Startled, she both heard and felt Ray say the short, accusing sentence.

Her mind scrambled around quickly, desperately trying to put a clearer meaning to his words, but she couldn't. She kept drawing a blank. Fear was holding all her thoughts prisoner.

"Tell you what?" Holly finally asked.

Again she felt his words rumbling against her cheek. "You know."

Holly raised her head to look at him. He wasn't teasing her or playing some guessing game. He looked serious and—unless her perception was off—uncomfortable, as well.

She knew it.

She just *knew* that when the heart-racing frenzy had lifted, Ray would be uncomfortable around her because they'd been intimate.

Was she going to lose his friendship because of her misstep?

Oh, God, how did she turn this around?

"If I knew," she said, her voice hardly above a whisper as she measured out her words, "I wouldn't be asking you what you meant. I don't play games, remember? How long have you known me?"

She was trying to use the time factor to her benefit, to remind him that they had been friends for years and years, and lovers for under an hour. With her head clearing, she didn't want to sacrifice their friendship for an exquisite hour of pleasure, no matter how wonderful it had been—and it had been *really* wonderful. But wonderful or not, she wanted Ray in her life beyond tonight.

Then you should have gone home, she upbraided herself angrily.

"How long have I known you?" Ray repeated. "I don't know. An hour, maybe less."

Now he had really lost her. *Was* this some game after all? "What are you talking about? You've known me for years and years."

"I *thought* I knew you for years and years," Ray corrected. "But obviously, I never did. This is a whole new side of you that I don't know. And you never once broached it," he pointed out.

"Broached *what?*" she cried. That she loved him? That she wanted to be with him? That she couldn't stand listening to him talk about other females when she ached to be the one in his arms? The one he made love with and wanted to have children with?

It took him several tries to tell her. Each time he began, it was as if his tongue went numb. "That you— That you were— That you were a virgin." He all but expelled the final word.

She stared at him. Was he complaining about her lack of experience? Had she wound up disappointing him in the end? Was *that* what this awkward conversation was about?

Exactly when did he think she should have announced that little piece of information? "Not exactly a conversation starter," she bit off as she struggled to sit up. Once upright, she reached for her discarded uniform on the floor. "I'm sorry I disappointed you."

"Disappoint—" He swallowed the rest of the word, stunned. "That's *not* what this is about," he told her, frustrated and angry at the same time. Frustrated with her for not telling him she was a virgin, angry at himself for what he'd just gone and done.

"Then what *is* this about?" she asked.

Didn't she understand? Why did he have to spell it out this way? "Damn it, Doll, I *took* something from you," he shouted. "I took your innocence, your virginity," he specified helplessly.

He wasn't feeling disappointed, he was feeling guilty, Holly suddenly realized.

"You didn't 'take' anything I didn't want to give you," she insisted. Taking a breath, she let her voice drop a couple of decibels. Maybe he just wanted her to sweep it all under the rug. She could oblige him— or pretend to.

"Look, what happened here happened. We'll just move on," she told him, praying that they could, that he wouldn't just distance himself from her the way he had from the other women he'd been involved with.

"Don't you understand?" he asked her, struggling *not* to take out his anger on her. "You should have told me you were a virgin."

Let it go, Ray, let it go. "In case you hadn't noticed, we weren't doing all that much talking at the time. Look, if you feel like you wasted your time, I get it. No words needed—"

"Wasted my time?" he repeated. "Holly, I wasted yours. Your first time should have been special."

She looked at him, knowing she was risking everything by what she was about to say to him. But knowing, too, that she had to be truthful with him. Being truthful was the definition of who and what she was. If she turned her back on that, she would be turning her back on her soul, as well.

Her eyes met his as she said, "It was."

She totally disarmed him. He had no idea what to say to her. All his fancy speeches, the charm he could pour on so effortlessly, it all deserted him, leaving him tongue-tied and totally confused.

She was his best friend. He'd just made love to his best friend. And he didn't even have a whisper of intoxication to blame it on.

This, he knew, was going to require a great deal of sorting out in the morning. And who knew if it *could* be sorted out? But right now, they were here, in this tiny back room, with nothing between them except the heat they'd just generated.

This wasn't the time to be going by the rule book. This was a time to start making up new rules.

"Miss Joan ever come back here after she's left for the night?" he asked her.

Holly thought for a moment, then shook her head. "Not that I know of," she confessed. "I've only closed up a couple of times before. She's never mentioned coming back. When she leaves for the day, Miss Joan spends the rest of the night with Harry. She's mentioned a couple of times that she feels like she's shortchanging him by working all those hours." She cocked her head as she looked at him. "Why?"

"Well," Ray responded, picking his words slowly— almost as slowly as he feathered his fingers through her hair, "I just wanted to be sure that we weren't going to have to go scrambling for our clothes because she's come back to the diner to get something."

"Well, there is always that chance, I suppose," she guessed, doing her best to hide the amused smile that rose to her lips.

It was going to be okay, her heart sang.

"How about it? Do you feel lucky?" Ray asked. He searched her face, trying to read her expression and match his words to it. But he couldn't quite delve beneath the layers. Was she teasing? Or serious?

"The way I see it," she told him, "I already am lucky."

"Okay." There was pure sensual mischief in Ray's brown eyes as he said, "So how about it? One for the road?"

"The road," she told him, bringing her mouth closer to his, "can take care of itself."

The next moment, there was no more room for words.

He wasn't clear if he'd started to kiss her or if she had made the move first and kissed him. All he knew was that their lips were suddenly, pleasurably, sealed to each other's.

Again.

Ray could feel himself instantly wanting her again, wanting her with an overwhelming desire that he'd never experienced to this heightened degree before. He knew, because of the circumstances, that this time around he should be more gentle, more tender with her, but he was more ravenous.

And all the while, a small, unbidden voice kept whispering over and over again, *This is Holly, your best friend, Holly. How long has this been going on without you suspecting it was there?*

Ray had no clue, and right now, he wasn't up to solving the mystery. All he wanted to do was to make love with her again, until he was finally, permanently satisfied, the way that he always had been before.

HE WASN'T GOING to get his wish, Ray thought darkly several days later. He wasn't going to be finally sated, finally satisfied so that he could just move on. The fact was becoming all too clear to him.

Because every time he made love with Holly— and they had managed to find a way to make love at least once every day since that first evening—all he wanted was to do it again.

And again.

And when he couldn't, he could only think about when he could.

What the hell has happened to you? he silently demanded, bewildered and frustrated as he tried to work off his tension by baling hay behind the main barn.

That was where Rafe found him.

Rather than yell out a greeting, Gabe's twin brother stood in silence for a few minutes, watching a man who strongly resembled his carefree youngest brother take out whatever was bothering him on the bales of hay.

"The hay do something to offend you, brother?" Rafe finally asked as he stepped forward to join Ray.

Ray paused, the pitchfork grasped in his hands suspended in midthrust. He slanted a dismissive glance in Rafe's direction. "What the hell are you talking about?" he asked, struggling not to snap the words out at Rafe.

"Well," Rafe began expansively, "you're wielding that pitchfork as if you're intent on stabbing each bale of hay before it gets the drop on you. I was just wondering if they did something to offend you—or if you've been nipping at your own private stock of whiskey a little early today."

Ray was having enough trouble dealing with his feelings and this unfamiliar situation he found himself in—he'd never wanted a woman *more* after having her. It had always been the law of diminishing returns for him, not this. Having to put up with Rafe's off-kilter sense of humor was just asking too much of him.

"Don't you have anything better to do than watch me pitch hay?" Ray demanded.

"No, not at the moment. This is pretty entertaining," Rafe confessed. And then he became serious. "Something bothering you, Ray?" he asked.

Ray glared at his brother. "Other than you?"

His brother inclined his head. "That was implied, yes."

"Then no," Ray bit out. The next hard thrust sent not just the hay flying, but the pitchfork, as well. Ray swallowed a curse, then sent another glare in Rafe's direction. "Not a word," he warned.

"Just an observation," Rafe couldn't resist saying. "You get more done if you hold on to the pitchfork."

Stomping over to where the pitchfork had landed, Ray snatched it up and stomped back to where he'd been working.

"Maybe I'll get more done if I use it on you and get you to shut up."

"That's not going to solve your problem, Ray."

"*You're* my problem, Rafe," Ray snapped.

"No," Rafe contradicted, then explained to his brother, "I'm what my wife calls 'the Greek chorus.'"

Rafe spared him another annoyed look. "What the hell is that?"

"Some kind of a writer's device they used back in the day. It's to summarize for the audience what's going on in case somebody who's watching loses track. They put things into words."

"You ask me, you're already using too many words as it is," Ray snapped, turning his back again.

Rafe shifted so that he was standing in front of his youngest brother, not letting him avoid eye contact.

"Look, we don't spend enough time together any-more, and pretty soon there'll even be less time avail-able, what with all of us getting married and such. Don't waste what little time we have by pretending everything's okay with you. Word is that you're not tomcatting around anymore. Wanna tell me what's up?"

"Not particularly," Ray said coldly, trying to ig-nore Rafe again.

"Tell me anyway." This time, it didn't sound like a request so much as an order.

Tempted to tell his brother what he could do with his suggestion, Ray reined himself in and just barked, "I'm busy."

"You were *never* too busy for female companion-ship, even when you were in first grade. Now, what's up?" Rafe demanded, looking at his brother more closely.

"You've met somebody," he suddenly realized.

"Somebody serious," Rafe concluded. "And you're scared to death."

"Now who's drinking?" Ray asked, even as he turned away from Rafe. His brother was getting too close to the truth, and Ray had no desire to go into it at length or even just discuss it fleetingly.

But Rafe circled so that his youngest brother couldn't avoid him. "Look me in the eye and tell me there's nobody serious."

Ray pressed his lips together, anger flaring in his eyes. "There's nobody serious," he bit off.

Unconvinced, Rafe shook his head and declared, "Liar."

Fed up, Rae thrust the pitchfork handle at his brother. "Since you're here and you seem to have all this time on your hands, *you* pitch hay for a while."

"While you go visit your mystery lady?" Rafe asked.

"No," Ray countered. "While I go and look up the name of a good head shrinker in Pine Ridge, because you clearly are in need of one." With that, he stormed off in the direction of the house.

"Who are you bringing to Mike's wedding?" Rafe asked, calling after him.

"Holly." The answer came spontaneously, before Ray could think things through and realize the trap that he'd just walked into.

"Damn," Rafe cried, stunned. And then he grinned from ear to ear. "Holly, huh? I'm slipping. I should have realized it sooner."

Ray squared his shoulders like a man about to do battle, but instead, he forced himself to just keep walking. "Nothing to realize," he snapped out, trying to sound indifferent and detached.

But it was too late. Rafe saw through the smoke screen. "If you say so, Ray."

He heard Rafe laughing to himself. Ray picked up his pace. Protesting what Rafe was alleging would only make things worse.

For everyone.

Chapter Sixteen

She wasn't sure, until he turned up on her doorstep, whether or not Ray *would* come to take her to his brother Mike's wedding.

Unofficially, of course, the whole town was invited, and she could have gone to both the ceremony and the reception without any problems. No one would have said anything, especially after she'd delivered Alma and Cash's twins.

But Ray had talked about their going together before they had become lovers, and she didn't know if, after their relationship had taken this unexpected turn, he would still want her there, or if being with her in public would make him feel awkward somehow.

And, as much as she wanted to attend the ceremony and reception, and as much as she cared about all of his siblings, she didn't want to be there if Ray didn't want her there.

So when she heard the doorbell ring, Holly froze before the mirror on her closet door, unable to make a single move because her knees had suddenly ceased functioning.

"I'll get it!" Molly called out, the sound of her little

feet rushing across the living room to the front door reinforcing her declaration.

"No, you won't, young lady," Holly heard her mother call out, then order, "You stop right there."

Granted, this was Forever and doors were left unlocked because everyone knew everyone else. But obedience was as highly prized here as anywhere else, and Molly had been taught not to open the door unless either her grandmother or her aunt was with her.

Martha pushed her salt-and-pepper hair out of her eyes. Moving quickly in her wheelchair, she reached the door just as Molly came to a skidding halt. The little girl looked at her grandmother, shifting impatiently from foot to foot, her little fingers wrapped around the doorknob.

"Now Grandma? Can I open the door *now?*"

The still youthful-looking woman maneuvered her wheelchair, bringing it to a halt right by her granddaughter. Only then did she say, "Now."

Molly yanked the door opened with both hands. "Aunt Holly, it's Ray," she called out at the top of her four-year-old lungs. "He looks really pretty, too," the little girl added, punctuating her statement with a giggle she tried to stifle with her hands.

"Well, thank you," Ray said in his best courtly manner. "This is for you," he added, holding out a gaily wrapped package. "I just passed this jolly-looking little fat man in a red suit and he asked if I could give it to you." Ray looked at her solemnly, as if he was quoting chapter and verse of a legal statement. "Said you were extragood this year so he couldn't carry all your presents at once. Told me he'd be back when you were asleep with the rest of them."

Molly's mouth dropped open as her eyes grew huge. "You saw Santa Claus?" she asked in hushed disbelief. "Really?" Disbelief turned to delight as she eyed the gift Ray had in his hands.

"Was that who it was?" Ray asked, looking at her in surprise. Then he nodded his head, as if he'd reviewed the evidence in his mind. "I guess it was, at that. Those prancing reindeer he had with him should have given it away, huh?"

"He had his reindeer with him?" Molly echoed, beside herself with excitement. She looked as if she was going to begin jumping up and down at any minute. "What did they look like?"

"Like their pictures," Ray answered, smoothly getting out of offering a description he wasn't prepared to render.

"Aunt Holly, Aunt Holly," Molly called out when she apparently heard Holly coming down the hallway. "Look what Santa Claus gave me. A present! Can I open it, *please?*" she begged.

But it was Martha who answered when she saw Holly wavering. "You know the rules, Molly. Any Christmas present you get goes under the tree until Christmas morning."

Molly sighed mightily, as if the weight of the world was on her shoulders, forcing her to behave like a responsible adult even when she didn't want to.

After another sigh, she finally agreed. "Okay, I'll wait." Molly looked far from happy about having to follow through with the statement.

"That's a good girl," Martha told her, lightly patting Molly's head.

Neither Molly nor Martha looked as if they were

dressed to attend the ceremony. Ray looked from one to the other before asking, "You two ladies aren't going to the wedding?"

Martha shook her head. "Between the ceremony and the reception, we'd wind up coming home way passed Molly's bedtime. And besides," she interjected, "I don't want Holly spending all her time at the wedding wheeling me around." Martha slanted a warm look at her daughter, then shifted her eyes from Holly to Ray. "She deserves to have a little fun instead of being stuck playing nanny to someone twice her age."

"Pushing you around in the wheelchair isn't a hardship, Mom," Holly protested.

"Well, it certainly doesn't come under the definition of having fun," Martha insisted. "Ray, would you please get her out of here before she starts to badger me?"

"You heard your mother," Ray said, pointedly offering Holly his arm.

Aware of every single one of Ray's actions as if they were transpiring under a high-powered magnifying glass, Holly slipped her arm through his, feeling as if she was moving in slow motion.

"Have fun, you two. That's an order," Martha Johnson instructed as she wheeled herself to the door in their wake and closed the door behind them.

"You look really, really good tonight," Ray told her as he held the passenger door of his freshly washed truck open for her.

It was dusk, and Holly was extremely grateful that the partial darkness hid the annoying blush that she could feel speedily taking possession of her cheeks. She was *really* going to have to work to get that under control, she lectured herself. She wasn't a starry-eyed twelve-year-old, she was a woman, and women didn't blush in this day and age. Even women who were wildly head over heels in love.

"Thank you," she murmured. "So do you." Getting in, she buckled up and waited for Ray as he rounded the hood and got in on the driver's side. "I wasn't sure you were going to come pick me up."

"Why not?" he asked, puzzled as he started up the truck. "I said I would." Pulling the truck away from the front of the house, he turned the vehicle around and stepped down on the accelerator.

Holly avoided his eyes, looking instead at the knotted hands in her lap. "I know, but that was before."

"Before?" What was she talking about? For the most part, he and Holly understood one another— mainly because she didn't retort to *female speak,* something he'd found most women did when they wanted to utterly confuse the man they were talking to. "Before what?"

"Before you and I…" Holly paused, searching for the right, delicate way to word this. She finally settled on, "Got close."

She was obviously not getting through because, in all innocence, Ray reminded her, "We've always been close."

"Not *this* close," she stressed.

The light finally dawned in his head and Ray laughed as he drove them to the church where the wedding ceremony was to take place.

"You have a point, but that still doesn't change the

fact that you're my best friend and after the way you came through for Alma, my father would probably skin me alive if I didn't bring you to the wedding— or if I turned out to be the reason you decided not to show up." He glanced in her direction. "You do want to attend, don't you?" he asked. "I mean, what's going on between us isn't going to make you feel uncomfortable going to the wedding, right?"

It had never occurred to her that Ray might see the situation from her perspective, thinking that *she* might not want to be around him rather than the other way around.

Could Ray possibly feel…insecure?

It hardly seemed likely. And yet, how else could she explain that the man whose relationships lasted only slightly longer than the life expectancy of a fruit fly was concerned that *she* might not want to continue this part of their relationship because it made her uncomfortable to be around him?

"No," Holly replied quietly but firmly. "What's going on between us doesn't make me feel uncomfortable around your family. I just don't want to cramp your style," she told him for lack of a better way to phrase her reason for thinking he might not come for her.

"My style," he echoed, the corners of his mouth curving at the phrase she'd used. "About that," he began, then paused.

"Yes?" she asked, silently urging him to continue even as she wondered if she'd ultimately regret finding out what he meant.

She was well aware that once things were said, they couldn't be unsaid. And, as long as they *weren't* said, she could go on pretending that everything in Paradise was just perfect. Even though "perfect" was a condition that in all likelihood didn't really exist.

Oh, God, when had life gotten so very complicated? Holly couldn't help wondering.

"Just exactly what is my style, Holly?" he asked.

She shrugged, fidgeting inside. "You're the charmer, the smooth talker, the one who all the unattached—and not so unattached—women gravitate to." He knew that, didn't he? Why was he asking her to spell it out? "What's the matter, Ray, your ego need a boost? Is that why you're asking me to define your style? You afraid that lingering with me might disturb some sort of equilibrium you have going out there in the universe?"

"What the hell are you talking about?" he asked her, completely confused.

Holly was being honest with him. She'd known Ray far too long not to be, and besides, she didn't know how to be anything else *but* straight. There wasn't—and never had been—a single conniving bone in her body.

She ran her tongue along exceedingly dry lips before she told him, "I'm waiting for the shoe to drop."

"What shoe?" he asked, no clearer now as to her meaning than he had been a moment ago.

"*The* shoe," she emphasized. Didn't he get it? "The proverbial shoe."

"What the hell is the proverbial shoe? Those online courses you're taking scrambling your brain?" he demanded, clearly frustrated that he didn't understand what she was trying to say. "I'm a plain man, Holly, talk plain."

She opened her mouth to answer him, and then shut it again as she stared at Ray. Holly. He'd called her Holly. Not Doll the way he usually did, but Holly. She couldn't remember the last time she'd heard him use her given name.

Was that a good sign, or should she *really* be bracing herself for something serious?

Something bad?

"The proverbial shoe," she repeated, then went on to add, "Everything that goes up must come down. For every good, there's a bad. If there's a high point, there has to be a low—am I making myself clear?" she asked, her voice rising.

Almost at the church, he suddenly pulled over so that he could focus completely on this conversation that wasn't making any sense to him. Maybe if he wasn't distracted by driving, it would become clearer.

"If by clear, you mean do I notice that you're talking in clichés as well as going around in circles, then, yes, I get that. I also know that of the two of us, you're supposed to be the optimist and I'm the one who's supposed to shoot down all your red balloons or the bluebird of happiness, or whatever it is that pessimists fantasize about doing to optimists to get them to reverse their opinions. But I'm not feeling any of that," he insisted, then quietly admitted, "I am, though, feeling a little confused because I've never been on this path before."

"You're going to have to be more specific than that, Ray," she told him. "What path?"

He'd already said too much, Ray upbraided himself.

He would have laughed if it wasn't all so damn

ironic. Normally, this was a conversation he'd be having with his best friend—with her—about the way he was feeling about the woman he was currently seeing. But in this case, his best friend and the woman he was currently seeing were one and the same, making all of this immensely complicated for him.

He'd always laid his soul bare to his best friend, but never to the woman he was dating.

Ray sighed, dragging his hand through his hair, trying hard to sort out his thoughts. It really didn't help.

He started up the truck, fully aware that Holly was staring at him. Waiting for him to continue.

He was going to have to handle and sort out this problem himself. Later.

"Never mind," he said, tabling the subject indefinitely. Focusing, he suddenly realized that they were almost on top of the church. "We're here," he announced, making it seem that he wasn't going to go into any lengthy explanation about what was going on inside his head because they had arrived at his brother's wedding. "Don't want to be late," he added quickly as he got out of the truck.

By her watch, they were a good fifteen minutes early, but she wasn't about to point that out. The last thing in the world she wanted to do was to come across as pushy. She was going to do her damnedest to continue being his best friend—except even better, she thought.

And what? He's going to get so overwhelmed by you, by how great you are, and so carried away by Mike's wedding that he's going to propose to you?

*Wake up and smell the rejection that's coming, Holly.
It's the only way you're going to survive.*

But she knew that she didn't want to survive. Not
just survive. She wanted to be his best friend *and* the
woman he came home to at night—or, at least, the
woman he wanted in his bed.

Dream on, an annoying little voice in Holly's head
mocked.

That was probably the right term for it, she thought,
making her way into the church beside Ray. A dream.
That was all she had and all she ever would have.

No matter what she wished to the contrary, Ray
Rodriguez was not the marrying kind. He'd told her
only a few weeks ago, when Mike said he planned to
marry Samantha on Christmas Eve, that he thought
his brothers were surrendering their freedom one by
one and he considered Mike to be the last bastion of
bachelorhood. With Mike's fall, he was the very last
standard-bearer.

Standard-bearers did *not* get married, not when
they considered themselves the epitome of bachelorhood. Besides, it was a known fact that Ray always
had too much fun being single and in demand. What
man who had all that going for him would want to
give it up for just one woman?

She knew the answer to that.

No man would. At least, not Ray. And she really
couldn't fault him for it.

Which meant she was going to enjoy this interlude
she was sharing with Ray and have absolutely no ex-
pectations, cast no webs, twine no strings.

This was what it was: decidedly wonderful—and,
in all likelihood, decidedly fleeting.

With that in mind, she stood up in the pew, brought to her feet by the beginning strains of "Here Comes the Bride."

And as she listened, she tried very hard to suppress the tears that rose to her eyes due to the sharp, painful realization that this song would never be played for her.

Chapter Seventeen

Because the weather promised to be colder than they had originally anticipated, it had been decided the day before the actual wedding to shift the site of Mike and Sam's reception to the Rodriguez ranch.

Those guests who were hearty enough not to be bothered by a little drop in temperature celebrated outside, directly behind the ranch house, where several canopies were set up—brought in for the occasion thanks to Rafe's wife, Valentine, and her connections with the movie industry where the use of canopies on location shots was commonplace.

Guests of a slightly more delicate constitution celebrated the wedding indoors, easily filling the house to overflowing with their bodies and their laughter.

Faced with the choice, Holly stayed outdoors, where a blanket of stars made the evening seem even more special than it already was. That, and the fact that Liam Murphy's band had set up outside—close enough to the house to be heard inside, but really resonating outdoors.

To her surprise, rather than mingling and disappearing, Ray had stayed with her for the entire evening, despite the blatant efforts of more than one woman to catch his eye.

It was, all in all, an enchanted evening as far as Holly was concerned. But even fairy tales ended, so this evening had to, as well. She had somewhere to be after midnight.

"You keep looking at your watch," Ray noted as he brought her another glass of punch. "Is there something I should know?"

She'd really tried not to be obvious about it, and she hadn't thought that he'd even noticed. The man was more aware of things than she gave him credit for.

"Like what?" she asked innocently.

"Like that you turn into a pumpkin at midnight. You know, the Cinderella thing," he prompted with a grin. He felt himself getting nervous, wondering if maybe he'd misread the signs after all. Was she anxious to leave the reception—and him?

"No," Holly said, "I'm not turning into a pumpkin, but I do want to be home around that time so I can get the rest of Molly's presents under the tree before she wakes up. Christmas Eve, she sleeps with one ear open, trying to catch Santa Claus in the act," she told him with a laugh. "By the way, that was a very nice thing you did, bringing Molly that gift and telling her it was from Santa."

He shrugged casually, dismissing the deed. "Well, I'm a very nice guy."

You don't have to convince me, Holly thought. *I've always been your biggest fan.*

Out loud she said, "You didn't have to do that, you know."

"I know." The truth of it was that he enjoyed it. "There's just something magical about that age, about believing in Santa Claus and an old man who can bring toys to everyone in one night."

"To all the kids in one night," Holly corrected.

About to continue, trying to warm to his real subject, he stopped abruptly. "What?"

"You said *to everyone*," she pointed out. "Santa is just supposed to bring gifts to the kids."

Ray frowned, his brow furrowing. "Is that written down somewhere?" he asked her, looking so solemn that for a second, she thought he was serious.

And then she realized that he was just pulling her leg, the way he always did, and she laughed. "It must be."

"Well, I never saw it written anywhere," he continued as if they were having a philosophical discussion. "And until I do, I'll keep on believing that Santa Claus is supposed to bring gifts to everyone."

Holly shook her head. "Just how much beer and wine have you had tonight?" she asked.

He looked at her for a long moment. The noise around them seemed to fade into the distant background as he told her quietly, "Just enough to make me see things a little more clearly than I normally do."

He was dragging this out a little, but she just *knew* there was going to be some kind of a punch line at the end.

"Uh-huh. You just keep thinking that." Holly glanced at her watch again. It was getting really close to midnight. She had to get going before she was completely dead on her feet. "Well, it's been a lovely night and a beautiful ceremony, but I'm going to have to ask you to take me home. Or better yet," she said, looking around the immediate area, "maybe I'd better ask one of the Murphy brothers to do it."

"One of the Murphy brothers?" Ray echoed, frowning. "Why?"

Granted, Ray didn't smell as if he'd been drinking, but something was off. He wasn't acting like himself tonight, and she just assumed it was because he'd had a bit to drink. She didn't want him taking any chances.

"Well, Brett and Liam don't seem to be drinking," she told him, "and even if we're not anywhere near the heart of Dallas, it's still safer to face the road stone-cold sober—especially at night."

Ray caught her hand, threading his fingers through hers. When she looked at him quizzically, he told her, "There's still plenty of time to get you home," he assured her. "A few more minutes won't make a difference in the grand scheme of things." The next moment, as she began to open her mouth in what he anticipated to be protest, he coaxed, "Dance with me."

"There's no music," Holly pointed out.

Ray held up his free hand. "Wait for it," he told her, cocking his head and following his own advice.

If she'd only had herself to consider, she would have stood right here beside him until the world ended. But she had Molly to think of and that changed everything. "Ray, I really have to—"

"See? There it is," he told her as Liam's band, returning from their fifteen-minute break, began to play again. It was a slow, bluesy number that Ray thought was just perfect. "You just have to be patient," he told her, drawing her out onto the dance floor that he and his brothers had just constructed for the occasion yesterday. It had taken all of them working together to make it a reality overnight. But that was the kind of thing he and his brothers did—the impossible in a short amount of time.

He took comfort in that now.

"Now that's funny," she said as she began to relax a little and follow his lead.

Ray looked intently into her eyes, allowing himself to get lost there just for a moment. "What is?"

"You telling me to be patient." *I've been patient all my life, Ray, waiting for you to notice me for just a little while.*

His mouth curved a little, despite his attempt to sound as if he was serious when he asked, "Are you hinting that I'm impatient?"

"No, not hinting," she countered with a laugh that filtered into her eyes. "Saying it outright."

"Maybe I was," he allowed magnanimously. "But that was the old me. The new me is very patient," he informed her.

Yeah, right. Never happen. But for the sake of peace, she played along. "And what is this 'new you' being so patient about?" she asked, doing her best not to laugh at him saying his name in the same sentence as the word *patient.* Everyone knew he was mercurial and the very definition of impatient.

She'd understand better afterwards, he decided. "Why don't we get back to that later?"

"Okay," she agreed, convinced that when "later" came, he will have forgotten all about it, which would have been typical Ray. Charmingly absentminded.

It wasn't that he was deliberately telling a lie, he

just wasn't able to keep track of everything that he'd said. That was part of who he was and she accepted that, accepted it all, just as long as she could have these precious moments with him to savor and relive later in her mind until she had worn off all the edges on her memories.

I'm never going to forget any of this, God. Thank You, she thought.

"It's almost Christmas Day," Ray told her, as if searching for the words that he needed.

"I know," she told him quietly. "I pointed that out to you. That's why I need to get home."

"You don't open presents until it's Christmas Day, right?" he asked her out of the blue.

"It's a tradition," she explained. "When you don't have much, you like to stretch out the drama a little, stare at your gift and imagine what it could be." She wondered if he was asking why her mother had told Molly to put his gift under the tree rather than allowing her to open it right then and there. "Mom and I both spoil Molly, but it won't hurt her to wait a bit, the way I did."

"I never realized that you were actually poor," he confessed.

"I didn't feel poor," she told him quickly, not wanting him to think this was some sort of a ploy for sympathy. "It was just in hindsight, looking back over everything, that I realized I didn't have as much— materially speaking—as some of the other kids. But on the plus side," she added, because she always tried to find the positive in any situation, "it made me stronger and less materialistic."

"So presents don't matter?" he asked her innocently.

She laughed. If there was one thing Ray wasn't, it was innocent.

"Now, I didn't say that. They matter," she admitted freely. "Because I'm not expecting them and because no one has an obligation to give me anything." There was something in his eyes she couldn't fathom. She didn't like not being able to read him. "What's all this talk about gifts?" she asked despite herself. The right thing would have been to allow him to talk and then drop the subject when he stopped. But her curiosity had gotten the better of her.

What if he's feeling you out and wants your advice about giving some girl a gift at midnight? An important gift at midnight?

Rather than answer, he went on dancing with her, raising his eyes to the old clock that was mounted on the back wall of the ranch house as they spun by.

The music ended just as the clock struck twelve.

"It's midnight," she told him needlessly.

He glanced over his shoulder at the clock out of habit. "Yes, it is."

"Now can I go home?" she pressed. As much as she loved being in his arms, dancing like this, she had to tear herself away—before she couldn't.

"In a minute," he told her. "I need to show you something."

Holly struggled to suppress the sigh that rose within her of its own accord.

She was right.

He had a gift for some other girl and wanted her

opinion on it. She needed to leave. Why hadn't he shown it to her earlier?

Seriously? Is that what you would have really wanted? To spend the entire evening knowing that he was here with you like this just out of friendship, and the woman he really wanted to spend time with was going to get a special Christmas gift while you found your own way home?

"Where are we going?" she asked as he walked beyond the canopies. Within moments, they had left the reception behind them.

He wanted to keep going until they were all alone. But then they would also run out of light because, as star filled as the sky was, it still didn't afford that much actual light. And he wanted her to be able to see what he had to show her—as well as wanting to see her expression when she saw it.

He hoped to God that he wasn't going to regret this.

"Here," he told her, stopping. "We're going here."

She looked around. They were practically out in the open field. She looked back at him uncertainly. "What's here?" she asked.

"We're here," he told her simply.

"I kind of figured that part out," she told him, waiting to hear just what was going on. When he hesitated, she looked at him with concern. He'd never had trouble telling her anything before.

Was this going to hit her hard? she suddenly wondered, bracing herself. Whatever it was, anticipation was making it far worse. She wanted to get it over with, like ripping a Band-Aid off an open wound.

"Is something wrong?" she asked, her throat so dry she was having trouble talking.

"Well," he said slowly, "that all depends."

"On what?" she asked him, surprised that she could actually get the words out despite the fact that they were sticking to the inside of her throat.

His eyes held hers. Time seemed to stand still, he noticed. "On what you say."

She stared at him. Since when did her opinion matter *that* much? Oh, he usually asked her what she thought, but the truth was he was his own man and did whatever he wanted to in the end.

Her saying no wasn't going to matter, so why was he going through this charade?

But she played along. "Okay," she told him gamely. "I'm ready."

"I hope so," he replied, only managing to compound her confusion.

Before she could ask him what that was supposed to mean, he put his hand into his pocket and pulled out something small. "Here," he said, thrusting out his hand and opening it.

She stared at the small square velvet box in the palm of his hand.

"Here what?" she whispered. She willed herself not to cry, but even now she could feel her eyes sting. Having her approve a ring for someone else was downright cruel.

"Here," he repeated more urgently. "Open it."

She felt her heart plummet to her toes. Her moment with him was over. She wasn't ready for it to be over, but it was. Just like that.

Forcing herself to take the ring box from him, she

opened it. Inside was the most beautiful diamond ring she'd ever seen. It managed to capture the moonlight, defusing it through the cluster of small diamonds, bouncing it off the large marquis shape in the middle.

"Well?" he asked impatiently. It clearly had taken her breath away. Why wasn't she saying anything?

"It's beautiful," she whispered in a very shaky voice.

"But?" he asked, hearing the slight note of hesitation in her voice.

She looked at him, mystified. "But nothing. It's beautiful," she repeated. Taking a long breath, she raised her eyes to his again. "Who's it for?"

His jaw almost dropped open. "You're serious?" he asked, stunned.

Her eyes were stinging more than ever. It was only a matter of time before the tears began falling. She needed to be out of his sight by then.

"Please don't play games with me, Ray. Yes, I'm serious. Who's it for?"

"You, you idiot." *How could she not get that?* he couldn't help wondering.

"I'm not being an idiot," Holly shot back indignantly. "I'm— Me?" she cried as his words suddenly registered and sank in. She stared at him, her jaw slack. "You're giving *me* the ring?"

Why did she think he'd handed it to her? "Yes," he insisted.

Anyone else would have been jumping up and down for joy, assuming that the ring was for them— but she wasn't anyone else, and neither was Ray. Everything needed to be spelled out before she allowed any of her feelings to emerge.

"Why?"

She *still* needed explanations? This was harder than he'd thought—but then, Holly was worth it. "Because I thought you'd want to be traditional about this."

"This?" she asked, still refusing to embrace the obvious out of fear of being humiliated and hurt.

Ray could only stare at her. He wasn't being vague— Why was she giving him so much flack?

"Why are you making this so difficult?" he asked. "I'm asking you to marry me."

She almost lost the ability to talk just then—but then it came back to her. "No, you're not. What you are is confusing me. There's been no mention of marriage." Her head began to spin wildly as her heart beat so hard, she thought she was just going to pass out. "You're actually asking me to marry you?"

"Yes!" he shouted. "Finally!" he added with relief. He was beginning to think she was never going to get his meaning.

"Why?"

The question was almost as bad as her not getting it. "What do you mean why?"

"Why?" she repeated. "It's a perfectly clear three-letter word. Why are you asking me to marry you?" she asked. "Did you have too much to drink, or do you have some kind of bet going that you could get married at midnight, or—"

"It's because I love you, damn it," he shouted at her. "I love you and I realized these past couple of weeks that I've been wasting my time, going from woman to woman when I've got all the woman I'll ever need right here next to me."

He held her gaze for a moment, his eyes searching hers, looking for some sort of a sign of commitment, a note of validation.

"You're my best friend and I can't stop thinking about you. I don't *want* to stop thinking about you. Ever," he emphasized. "Marry me, Holly."

He was asking her to marry him. He was *really* asking her to marry him. This wasn't a dream. "When?" she asked.

"Whenever you're ready. Now, if you want me to go get the preacher," he told her eagerly, ready to pull the man out of his home behind the church.

"Wait, wait, this is going too fast." Part of her still expected to wake up at any second. "At the risk of ruining something I've wanted ever since I first saw you, I have to tell you something." She took a breath before adding, "You need to know that you're not just marrying me."

"I'm not?" Just exactly what was she getting at?

"No. I've got responsibilities, Ray. I've got Molly to take care of. I can't just turn my back on her."

Was that all? He got a kick out of the little girl. For one thing, he could talk to her. That wasn't always the case with kids Molly's age. "Not asking you to."

"And then there's my mother," Holly went on nervously. She didn't want to chase him away, but her responsibilities were what they were. "She's independent and stubborn, but I can't just leave her on her own."

"I know that." He grinned. "I like your mother. I know that she kind of likes me, too. And she said you'd be stubborn about this, but to keep after you until I wore you down."

"Wait." Something wasn't making sense here. "You talked to my mother about this?" she asked, stunned.

"Yeah." The conversation had been lengthy. "Why do you think she didn't come to the wedding? She didn't want you distracted, taking care of her, looking after Molly. I've got her blessing, by the way," he told her. "What I need now is yours."

Did he really think he had to ask? "You've had that all along," she told him. Without a need to restrain them, her tears fell freely.

"You're not supposed to cry when you say yes," he told her.

"Says who?" she sniffed.

"I don't know. Sounds like a good rule, though." He took her into his arms. "You're my everything, Holly, and I'm finally smart enough to realize that." It damn well took him long enough, he thought.

"If you're so smart, why haven't you shut up and kissed me yet?" she asked, challenging him.

"Just getting to the good part," he told her, bringing his mouth down to hers.

And it was the good part. The very best part of all. And he vowed that it would always remain that way.

Epilogue

Holly couldn't wait to tell them.

Couldn't wait to get home and tell her mother and Molly that she was going to marry the man she'd dreamed about marrying for most of her life.

Of course, there was a part of Holly that wanted to walk into her house and pretend that she'd decided to turn him down as a way of making her mother pay for having kept Ray's pending proposal a secret from her.

Her mother should have told her the second she knew.

But then she supposed she could see the argument for allowing Ray to be the one who actually asked her face-to-face. After all, it was his question, so he had to be the one who got to surprise her.

Hearing it come from his lips had kind of made the proposal rather perfect, Holly decided.

So she abandoned the idea of getting back at her mother by pretending that she had turned Ray down. For one thing, she truly doubted that she could fool her mother. She really wasn't *that* good an actress, especially not when her mother knew just how crazy she was, and always had been, about Ray.

Because she wanted to tell both her mother and

Molly at the same time, Holly knew that meant she needed to get home fairly early.

When she broached the matter to Ray to get his input, she was surprised by what he said.

"We don't have to leave the reception," Ray told her. "At least, not permanently, not if you don't want to."

"You mean, we should wait until morning to tell Mom and Molly?" she asked.

"No, I mean we can leave the reception temporarily. Take a break, like commercials being shown during some episode on TV. Just a quick break. It's not like we have to cross the state line to see your family."

Holly still hesitated for a moment, torn. After all, this was Ray's brother's wedding and she didn't want to seem rude or run the risk of offending anyone in his family. "You don't mind?"

"I don't mind anything that makes you happy," he told her simply.

Now that he had admitted to loving her, part of Ray couldn't help wondering what had taken him so long to come to his senses. What had taken him so long to see what was right in front of him.

He supposed that he should stop beating himself up about it and just be glad that he finally saw the light. End of story.

Or maybe, he couldn't help thinking with a grin, just the beginning of a new story.

"And your family won't mind?" she wanted to know.

"My family loves you, remember? You're the hero who brought Alma's twins into the world. *You* can do no wrong in their eyes."

He'd convinced her. "Okay," she said, taking Ray's hand in hers and leading him out toward where he'd parked his car. "Let's go."

HER HEART RODE shotgun in her throat all the way to her house, even though the trip seemed to be over in the blink of an eye.

The second Holly put her key into the front-door lock, it swung open. Martha was on the other side of it, her eyes bright, her expression a portrait of anticipation.

"Well?" Martha demanded, looking from one to the other expectantly. "Did you say yes?"

"Yes to what?" Molly wanted to know, hanging on to one of the wheelchair handles and attempting to swing herself to and fro. She was just small enough in weight and stature not to throw Martha off balance.

"You mean you don't know?" Holly asked with a laugh, stroking the little girl's hair.

"Uh-uh," Molly confirmed, then started chanting, "Tell me, tell me, tell me."

She told Molly gladly. With only minor coaxing, she would have yelled it out on a rooftop. "Ray and I are getting married."

The little girl surprised them all by looking very quietly and very solemnly from Holly to Ray, as if actually weighing what she'd just been told and subjecting that information to a number of criteria that she kept in her little head.

"Do you want to?" she finally asked Holly.

"Yes, I do. Very much," Holly told her niece.

Molly then looked at the man standing beside her

aunt and rather than ask the same question, asked instead, "Are you going to be moving in with us?"

"Looks that way. Is that okay with you?" he asked her, one adult to another, an attitude that Molly greatly appreciated.

When he asked her about her feelings on the matter, *that* was when her smile finally came out, a smile as big as a sunburst.

A smile that closely resembled the one he'd seen time and time again on Holly's lips.

"Yes!" Molly declared. "'Cause I really like my room and it would make me sad to leave it behind if I had to move away."

Ray dropped down to one knee to be on Molly's level. "Well, you're not going to be sad because we're not moving."

"Yeah!" Molly cried as she enthusiastically threw her arms around Ray's neck. "Can you marry us tomorrow?" she asked, turning it entirely into a family affair.

"It doesn't work that fast," he explained to Molly, talking to her as if he was talking to an adult. "But as soon as I can, I will."

Molly's eyes were shining as she nodded her approval. At the same time, she struggled to stifle a yawn. She was unsuccessful in the latter.

"Time for you to go to bed, young lady," Martha told her granddaughter. Just before she started to herd Molly from the room, using her wheelchair as effectively as any cowboy used his cattle pony, Martha glanced over at her daughter and her future son-in-law. "And why don't you two get out from underfoot and make yourselves scarce?" she ordered with a broad wink.

Ray took Holly's hand in his again. "I believe we've got a wedding reception to get back to," he said to her.

"You took the words right out of my mouth," Holly replied.

He grinned as they walked out of the house again. "Get used to it. I plan on doing that kind of excavation a lot."

She looked at him quizzically as the door closed behind them. "I don't think I understand—"

Rather than explain, he showed her by pulling her into his arms and sealing his mouth to hers. And just before he did, Holly, in a small, knowing voice, uttered an enlightened, "Oh."

The sound was muffled against his lips—which she could have sworn were smiling.

* * * * *

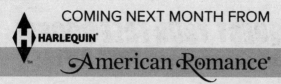
Available January 7, 2014

#1481 HER CALLAHAN FAMILY MAN
Callahan Cowboys
Tina Leonard

When Jace Callahan and Sawyer Cash engaged in their secretive affair, neither of them anticipated an unplanned pregnancy. Jace wants to seal the deal with a quickie marriage...but it turns out he has a very reluctant bride!

#1482 MARRYING THE COWBOY
Blue Falls, Texas
Trish Milburn

When a tornado rips through Blue Falls, good friends Elissa Mason and Pete Kayne find themselves sharing a house. Suddenly Elissa is thinking about her *pal* in a whole new way....

#1483 THE SURPRISE HOLIDAY DAD
Safe Harbor Medical
Jacqueline Diamond

Adrienne Cavill delivers other women's babies, but can't have one of her own. Now she may lose the nephew she's raising, and her heart, to his long-absent father, Wade Hunter. Unless the two of them can come up with a different arrangement?

#1484 RANCHER AT RISK
Barbara White Daille

Ryan Molloy's job is running his boss's ranch, so he doesn't have time to babysit Lianne Ward. She's there to establish a boys' camp—and definitely doesn't need Ryan looking over her shoulder every minute!

HARCNM1213

REQUEST YOUR FREE BOOKS!
2 FREE NOVELS PLUS 2 FREE GIFTS!

LOVE, HOME & HAPPINESS

YES! Please send me 2 FREE Harlequin® American Romance® novels and my 2 FREE gifts (gifts are worth about $10). After receiving them, if I don't wish to receive any more books, I can return the shipping statement marked "cancel." If I don't cancel, I will receive 4 brand-new novels every month and be billed just $4.74 per book in the U.S. or $5.24 per book in Canada. That's a savings of at least 14% off the cover price! It's quite a bargain! Shipping and handling is just 50¢ per book in the U.S. and 75¢ per book in Canada.* I understand that accepting the 2 free books and gifts places me under no obligation to buy anything. I can always return a shipment and cancel at any time. Even if I never buy another book, the two free books and gifts are mine to keep forever.

154/354 HDN F4YN

Name _____ (PLEASE PRINT)

Address _____ Apt. #

City _____ State/Prov. _____ Zip/Postal Code

Signature (if under 18, a parent or guardian must sign)

Mail to the **Harlequin® Reader Service:**
IN U.S.A.: P.O. Box 1867, Buffalo, NY 14240-1867
IN CANADA: P.O. Box 609, Fort Erie, Ontario L2A 5X3

Want to try two free books from another line?
Call 1-800-873-8635 or visit www.ReaderService.com.

* Terms and prices subject to change without notice. Prices do not include applicable taxes. Sales tax applicable in N.Y. Canadian residents will be charged applicable taxes. Offer not valid in Quebec. This offer is limited to one order per household. Not valid for current subscribers to Harlequin American Romance books. All orders subject to credit approval. Credit or debit balances in a customer's account(s) may be offset by any other outstanding balance owed by or to the customer. Please allow 4 to 6 weeks for delivery. Offer available while quantities last.

Your Privacy—The Harlequin® Reader Service is committed to protecting your privacy. Our Privacy Policy is available online at www.ReaderService.com or upon request from the Harlequin Reader Service.

We make a portion of our mailing list available to reputable third parties that offer products we believe may interest you. If you prefer that we not exchange your name with third parties, or if you wish to clarify or modify your communication preferences, please visit us at www.ReaderService.com/consumerchoice or write to us at Harlequin Reader Service Preference Service, P.O. Box 9062, Buffalo, NY 14269. Include your complete name and address.

HAR13R

*Their families may be rivals, but Jace Callahan
just can't stay away from Sawyer Cash!*

Jace Callahan appeared to be locked in place, thunderstruck. What had him completely poleaxed was that the little darling who had such spunk was quite clearly as pregnant as a busy bunny in spring.

She made no effort to hide it in a curve-hugging hot pink dress with long sleeves and a high waist. Taupe boots adorned her feet, and she looked sexy as a goddess, but for the glare she wore just for him.

A pregnant Sawyer Cash was a thorny issue, especially since she was the niece of their Rancho Diablo neighbor, Storm Cash. The Callahans didn't quite trust Storm, in spite of the fact that they'd hired Sawyer on to bodyguard the Callahan kinder.

But then Sawyer had simply vanished off the face of the earth, leaving only a note of resignation behind. No forwarding address, a slight that he'd known was directed at him.

Jace knew this because for the past year he and Sawyer had had "a thing," a secret they'd worked hard to keep completely concealed from everyone.

He'd missed sleeping with her these past many months she'd elected to vacate Rancho Diablo with no forwarding address. Standing here looking at her brought all the familiar desire back like a screaming banshee.

Yet clearly they had a problem. Best to face facts right up front. "Is that why you went away from Rancho Diablo?" he asked, pointing to her tummy.

She raised her chin. "It won't surprise me if you back out, Jace. You were never one for commitment."

Commitment, his boot. Of his six siblings, consisting of one sister and five brothers, he'd been the one who'd most longed to settle down.

He gazed at her stomach again, impressed by the righteous size to which she'd grown in the short months since he'd last seen her—and slept with her.

He wished he could drag her to his bed right now.

"I'm your prize, beautiful," he said with a grin. "No worries about that."

Look for HER CALLAHAN FAMILY MAN,
by USA TODAY bestselling author Tina Leonard
next month, from Harlequin® American Romance®.

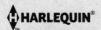

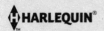

American Romance®

A fresh start

After the loss of his family in a tragic accident, Ryan Malloy has been given one last chance to change his life. His boss sends him to Flagman's Folly, New Mexico, to run his ranch, but unfortunately, Ryan's troubled attitude lands him in hot water with the ranch's gutsy project manager, Lianne Ward.

Deaf since birth, Lianne has never let her disability define her. But she's yet to meet a man who treats her as an equal. Ryan seems different…that is, when they're not butting heads.

Forced to work together, Lianne and Ryan discover an unexpected attraction beneath their quarreling. But will Ryan's painful past drive them apart…permanently?

Rancher At Risk

by BARBARA WHITE DAILLE

Available January 2014,
from Harlequin® American Romance®.

www.Harlequin.com

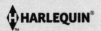

HARLEQUIN®

American Romance®

Friends, to roommates…to lovers?

Living with the Cupid of Blue Falls, Texas—her aunt
Verona—Elissa Mason should be married and pregnant
by now. Or so her friends tease. But Elissa's baby is the
family nursery. Following a devastating tornado, she has
to rebuild, and nothing's going to distract her. Not even
her strange, new feelings for neighbor-turned-roommate
Pete Kayne.

Deputy Sheriff Pete Kayne understands having a dream
and doesn't want to get in Elissa's way—especially after
the tornado has taken everything but his horse and his
friends. All he's got left to share is his heart. He has his
own ambition: a chance to join the ultimate in law
enforcement—the Texas Rangers. Elissa is his friend.
That will have to be enough…for now.

Marrying The Cowboy
by TRISH MILBURN

Available January 2014,
from Harlequin® American Romance®.

www.Harlequin.com

HAR75503

HARLEQUIN®

A *Romance* FOR EVERY MOOD™

Love the Harlequin book you just read?

Your opinion matters.

Review this book on your favorite
book site, review site, blog or your own
social media properties and share
your opinion with other readers!

Be sure to connect with us at:
Harlequin.com/Newsletters
Facebook.com/HarlequinBooks
Twitter.com/HarlequinBooks